MAKE MY DREAMS COME TRUE

The apartment was dark except for the multicolored lights on the tree, blinking in random patterns. The scent of evergreen filled the air. When he walked through the living room, the musical mistletoe triggered on, playing a tinny "Jingle Bells." Frances had bought him the whimsical gift only last week—an early Christmas present, she told him. More than anything, Booker had wanted to hold her under the mistletoe and give her the killer kiss of a lifetime.

But Frances was a friend and only a friend and he had commitments he hadn't quite ended. Yet. But he was working on that, and then he'd see to Frances. *Soon*, he promised himself. *Very soon.*

From He Sees You When
You're Sleeping

More from Lori Foster

LORI
FOSTER

GIVE IT UP

ZEBRA BOOKS
KENSINGTON PUBLISHING CORP.
http://www.kensingtonbooks.com

ZEBRA BOOKS are published by

Kensington Publishing Corp.
119 West 40th Street
New York, NY 10018

All Kensington titles, imprints, and distributed lines are available at special quantity discounts for bulk purchases for sales promotion, premiums, fund-raising, educational, or institutional use.

Special book excerpts or customized printings can also be created to fit specific needs. For details, write or phone the office of the Kensington Sales Manager: Attn.: Sales Department. Kensington Publishing Corp., 119 West 40th Street, New York, NY 10018. Phone: 1-800-221-2647.

Zebra and the Z logo Reg. U.S. Pat. & TM Off.

First Zebra Books Mass-Market Paperback Printing: December 2015
ISBN-13: 978-1-4201-3733-0
ISBN-10: 1-4201-3733-6

eISBN-13: 978-1-4201-3734-7
eISBN-10: 1-4201-3734-4

10 9 8 7 6 5 4 3 2 1

Printed in the United States of America

Dear Readers,

I love when my stories get new life by being reissued—most especially when related stories that were originally published in separate anthologies are put together under one cover.

Meet Booker, Cary, and Axel.

Booker and Axel are brothers and, as a very close friend, Cary is like a brother. I enjoyed writing each of these stories, but Axel's is one of my absolute favorites. I loved how outrageous he is and how, when needed, he always does the right thing.

If you're interested in seeing other reissued compilations, or just knowing which of my books are related, visit my website under the "Connected Books" link. lorifoster.com/connected-books

As always, I love hearing from readers and I'm accessible on most social-media outlets. Happy reading!

Lori Foster

CONTENTS

He Sees You When You're Sleeping

Chapter One

Booker Dean stood in front of his six-foot Christmas tree, gazing at the brightly lighted star atop and thinking of things that should be, but weren't. Yet.

The drive home had shown so many beautiful sights: laughing people laden with packages, store windows lavishly decorated, wreaths and lights and song. It was a magical time of the year, a time when anything seemed possible, a time when love became clearer, and he hoped, more attainable.

He'd only come in moments ago, had just hung his snow-dusted coat in the closet before going to the tree to think about her, to consider the task ahead of him. Resisting her was never easy, but in his present mood, it would be doubly hard. He was a man, and he wanted her, right now, this very instant. He wanted to share the magic of the holidays with her, today, tomorrow, for the rest of his life.

Did he dare approach her now, or should he wait until he was in better control?

Those thoughts got interrupted when his apartment door flew open without a knock. Booker strode to the entryway, saw his visitors and cursed. Damn it, he was too tired and edgy to have to put up with company from his brother tonight.

Axel hadn't come alone. He had his best friend Cary Rupert with him, and they both looked too serious.

Booker cocked one brow high. "Forgotten how to knock?"

"On my own brother's door?" Axel snorted, then shook himself like a mongrel dog, sending snow and ice around the foyer. It would be a white Christmas this year for sure, given the present weather and next week's forecast. "Besides," Axel continued, "I figured if you were doing anything private, you'd have the good sense to lock it."

"I just got in." Booker propped his hands on his hips and surveyed them both. Axel's dark brown eyes, much like his own, were strangely evasive. Cary unbuttoned his coat while casting worried glances toward Booker. Given the combined behavior of them both, misgivings surfaced. "All right. What's going on?"

Cary forestalled him by shivering and slapping at his arms. "You got anything hot to drink?"

Seeing no hope for it, Booker nodded. "Yeah sure." The apartment was dark except for the multicolored lights on the tree, blinking in random patterns. The scent of evergreen filled the air. When he walked through the living room, the musical mistletoe triggered on, playing a tinny "Jingle Bells." Frances had bought him the whimsical gift only last week—an early Christmas present, she told him. More than anything, Booker had wanted to hold her under the mistletoe and give her the killer kiss of a lifetime.

But Frances was a friend and only a friend and he had commitments he hadn't quite ended. Yet. But he was working on that, and then he'd see to Frances. *Soon,* he promised himself. *Very soon.*

Cary pulled a wooden chair away from the table and straddled it, crossing his arms over the back, his gaze still watchful. Axel went to stand by the sink. He rubbed his face tiredly and Booker realized he hadn't shaved.

At thirty, Axel was one year older than Booker, but ten times more outrageous. Where Booker had always wanted to settle down, buy a nice house and start a family, Axel seemed hell-bent on sowing wild oats till the day he croaked. He took his residency as a gynecologist seriously—despite all the teasing he got from male friends and family. But other than that, other than his chosen profession, Axel was a complete hedonist intent only on having fun and indulging desires.

Booker opened the cabinet door and pulled out a strong coffee blend; it looked like he was going to need it. "While I fix this, why don't you tell me why you look so glum."

Appearing more morose by the second, Axel groaned. "That's why I'm here, so I suppose I should. But God knows I hate to be the bearer of bad news. It's just that I figured you should hear it from me, not anyone else."

Booker paused. "Mom and Dad—"

Cary made a sound of exasperation. "Your family is fine and no one died. Jesus, Axel, just spit it out."

Axel pointed a finger at his friend. "You're here for moral support, so how about showing a little?"

Cary just rolled his eyes.

"Out with it, Axel." Booker threw in an extra scoop of coffee for good measure. "What did you do now?"

"I said no, that's what I did."

"No to what?"

"Not what, who."

"All right. Who?"

Visibly pained, Axel blurted, "Judith."

"Judith?" And then, with confusion, "My Judith?" Even as he said it, Booker winced. He didn't want her to be *his* Judith anymore. She was a sweet woman, very nice and innocent, but he wanted Frances. Hell, he'd been with Judith for five months now and . . . there was nothing. Just fizzle. Once Frances had moved in next door two months ago, he'd figured out what he really wanted in a woman, and Judith wasn't it.

But Frances was.

Axel pushed away from the sink. "Swear to God, Booker, I was just there minding my own business, burning off a little tension after a really long week."

Because Axel had raised his voice, and because Cary was busy nodding hard in agreement, Booker's suspicions grew. "You were just where?"

"At the bar. Hell, I was hitting on a redhead two seats down. She was hitting back, things were looking good, then suddenly Judith was there."

"Judith was at a bar?" That didn't sound like the Judith he knew.

"I think she was drunk, Booker," Cary explained in a rush. "She, uh, wasn't acting like herself. Said something about being tired of pretending."

Axel's Adam's apple bobbed and he said in agonized tones, "She grabbed my equipment, Booker. She just . . . grabbed it. I know you've been seeing her for a while now, but she's not who you think she is."

"She grabbed his equipment," Cary reiterated, still nodding.

"It was like . . ." Axel opened his hand over his fly and held himself firmly, making sure Booker understood. "Then she pressed up real close and breathed in my damn ear that she wanted me. *Me*, Booker." He shook his head in apology. "Not you."

Booker was so stunned, he reached back for a chair. Cary acted quickly, sliding one underneath his ass so he didn't hit the floor. "She grabbed you?"

"Like this." Still holding himself, Axel gave

his crotch a small shake. "I damn near swallowed my tongue and, well, hell, Booker. You can't hang onto a guy's equipment without getting a rise. I didn't mean to react. I even told her to let go. But she held on real tenacious like, even when I backed up. And backing up wasn't easy, I can tell you that. The place was jammed and that girl has a grip."

"He did say no," Cary assured him. "I was there, Booker. It was sort of a strangled whisper, a little garbled, but he said it. Only Judith didn't want to take no for an answer."

Booker looked between them. Scenarios played out in his mind in rapid succession. "Did you sleep with her then?"

"No!" Axel pulled back, horrified by the mere suggestion.

"Booker!" In his friend's defense, Cary was equally affronted. "You know your brother better than that."

It was all Booker could do not to laugh at the two of them, squawking like hens. He rubbed his jaw, bit back a grin, and said, "Axel, you can let go of yourself now."

"Oh. Yeah." Axel released his crotch and shoved his hands into his pockets. He hesitated, his frustration bubbling up until he started squawking again. "You had to know, Booker. I didn't want to be the one to tell you, but you had to know."

"Yep. I had to know."

Cary leaned toward him, filled with masculine concern. He clapped Booker on the back of the neck, gave him a too-tight squeeze. "You okay, Booker?"

"I'm fine actually." He shrugged off Cary's stranglehold, glanced up and saw the coffeemaker give one final hiss and spit. "Good, the coffee is done. You can each have one cup. I'll even let you have a Christmas cookie. Then I want you gone."

Axel and Cary looked at each other helplessly. "You upset?"

"Not really." Surprised. Exhilarated. But not upset. Booker filled three mugs to the top. None of them used sugar or cream, though Booker kept it on hand because Frances liked her coffee with plenty of both, and there were many a lazy Sunday morning where they shared a cup and talked about upcoming sports, work, or just sat together, doing nothing.

Well, Frances did nothing. Booker spent his time surreptitiously watching her, thinking about getting her out of her clothes, basically doing all the fantasizing men indulge in when with a woman they want. Bad.

He opened his cookie jar, took out a handful of the delicious, decorated cookies Frances had made for him, and set them on the table.

"What are you going to do, Booker?"

Booker shook off his musings. He noticed that Cary's brown hair was still damp from the sleet and snow. He pushed it back from his face while watching Booker with sympathy and concern. Hell, did they expect him to go ballistic?

To be furious with Axel? To sit around and mope with a broken heart?

This time he did laugh.

Cary leaned forward, and as a doctor, gave his professional opinion. "Damn, he's hysterical."

Axel's eyes widened. "Booker. Man, I swear I'm sorry. Judith is sweet on the eyes, no way around that. But I would never go behind your back—"

Knowing he had to put them at ease before they started trying to hug him or something equally unsavory, Booker set down his coffee. "You want to know what I'm going to do? Okay, I'll tell you. First, I'm going to shower and change into clean clothes. Then I'm going to go next door to see Frances. And then . . ." He savored the moment, his voice dropping to a husky drawl without him even realizing it. "Then, I'm going to make up for lost time."

Silence filled the kitchen until Axel fell back against the counter. "Frances?" he asked with some confusion.

Cary drew an incredulous face. "Your neighbor?"

"Yeah." In extreme anticipation, Booker rubbed his hands together. Frances might think of herself as just a friend for now, but that was about to change. The sooner the better.

When he got her naked and kissed her from head to toe, she'd understand he wanted more than friendship. A lot more—like everything.

"You're talking about that tall girl next door?" Cary asked, apparently needing clarification.

"The one who likes football and runs all the time?"

"She jogs, and yeah, she's the one." She'd been *The One* almost from the day he'd met her.

"I kinda thought she was gay," Cary confided.

Booker laughed. "No. She just doesn't date much because she's always working." Frances was a very talented artist, though so far most of her work centered around commissions for commercial outlets, like window paintings and murals in pediatrician and dentist offices. Recently, however, the local galleries had started showing her work—with much success.

"You got a thing for her?" Axel asked.

"Yeah. A thing. A big thing. Like a hard case of *gotta have her.*"

"No shit?" Axel grinned and for the first time that night, he relaxed. "Well, hell, that's great news, Booker." Then he thought to ask, "Does this girl feel the same about you?"

"Woman, and no. At least, not yet she doesn't. But then, we've done that damned disgusting platonic thing because she thought I was permanently tied to Judith and I was waiting until I could figure out how to end things with Judith without breaking her heart."

Cary choked. "I think her heart will be safe."

"It seems so." Booker was so relieved to have that particular problem solved that he couldn't wait to get to Frances. He turned to his brother. "I suppose I owe you a thank-you, for helping things along."

Axel fell into a thoughtful silence while sipping

his coffee. "So let me get this straight. You're not even the smallest bit upset that Judith was pawing me and licking on me?"

"Pawing you *and* licking you?"

Axel shrugged. "My ear and neck and stuff. She's got a hot little tongue on her, too. I thought for a minute there she was going to take a bite. And I had a helluva time getting her fingers off my zipper, but with the way she used that tongue, no way did I want my zipper down. She'd backed me damn near into the men's room and I swear, I thought the girl would molest me."

When Booker smiled, Cary added, "I've never seen your brother in such a panic, Booker. If I hadn't been worried about how you'd take it, I'd have been laughing my ass off."

"I'm not upset, Axel. This gives me the perfect out and I won't even have to be the bad guy."

Axel nodded, did some more thinking, then plunked down his coffee cup. "You know, Booker, I really wish you'd have let me in on all this *before* I told Judith no."

Cary snickered. "She was plenty pissed when you turned her down."

"Probably because she knows my brother never turns women down."

"Almost never," Axel specified. "But even I have to draw the line at women involved with my baby brother." He tipped his head at Booker. "Say, I don't suppose you'd care to give me her number?"

"God, Axel." Cary shook his head in disgust. "You're unbelievable."

Axel just smiled. "The way that girl held me was unbelievable. And since Booker doesn't mind, I figure why not?"

"I don't mind at all." Booker wrote down her number and handed it to Axel with his best wishes. "Good luck, and get out. I have things to do and they don't include the two of you."

"Given that look in your eyes, I should hope not," Cary said with a laugh.

Axel slung his arm around Booker on the way to the front door. He was twenty-five pounds heavier and an inch shorter than Booker, but other than that, the similarity in their appearance was uncanny. "So you think you'll be bringing Frances to Christmas dinner?"

With all his most immediate plans centered on getting her into bed, preferably tonight, he hadn't yet thought that far ahead. But it sounded like a hell of an idea. Frances was friendly, open, easy to talk to. If things worked out as he hoped, they'd be spending a lot of time together, especially during the holidays—and especially in bed. "I'll work on it."

Frances had paused in front of her tree to straighten a plump Santa ornament. The delicate glass reflected the white twinkly lights, looking almost magical. But there'd be no magic for her this year. What she wanted most, Santa couldn't put under her tree.

After working all day, she was hot and tired, and so when What-She-Wanted-Most knocked on her door, she almost jumped out of her skin.

She knew it was Booker, because she knew his knock, just as she knew his laugh, his tone of voice when he was excited, and his scent. God, she loved his scent.

With her heart swelling painfully, she opened the door with a false smile. As usual, he looked dark and sexy and so appealing, her pulse leaped at the sight of him.

Hands snug in his pockets, his flannel shirt open over a white thermal and nicely worn jeans, he leaned in her doorway. His silky black hair was still damp from a shower and his jaw was freshly shaved. He had a rakish "just won the lottery" look about him and the way he murmured, "Hi" had her blinking in surprise.

Somehow, he was different. There was a glimmer in his dark eyes, a special kind of attentiveness that hadn't been there only the day before. His gaze was direct and almost . . . intimate. Yeah, that was it. And he wore a funny little half smile of expectation.

Expectation of *what*?

Uncertainly, Frances managed a reply. "Hey, Booker. What's up?"

He stepped inside without an invite, but then, they were *friends* and Booker visited with her a lot. Whenever he wasn't working—or with Judith— he came by to play cards, watch sports, or just shoot the bull. Like he would with a pal.

Maybe it was the holidays making her nostalgic, but when she thought of being Booker's pal for the rest of her life, she wanted to curl up and cry.

A stray lock of hair had escaped her big clip and hung near her eyes. Taking his time and stopping her heart in the process, Booker smoothed it behind her ear.

No way in hell did he do that with his guy friends. She gulped.

In a voice low and gentle and seductive, he said, "What have you been doing that has you all warm on such a cold snowy day?"

Unnerved, Frances backed up out of reach. Booker stepped close again. "I, ah . . ." She gestured behind her. "I'm moving my room."

"Yeah?" He looked at her mouth. "Want to move it next door with me?"

She shook her head at his unfamiliar, suggestive teasing. "I'm switching my bedroom with my studio because the light is better in that room now."

As an artist, she liked to take advantage of whatever natural light she could get. In summer, she used her smaller guest bedroom for sleeping so that the larger room could be filled with her canvases and paints and pottery wheel. But now with winter hard upon them, the light was different. More often than not, long shadows filled the room, so she was switching. If nothing else, it gave her a way to fill the time rather than think of Booker and Judith snuggled up in front of a warm fire, playing kissy-face and more.

Booker stepped around her and closed the door. "Maybe I can help. What else do you have to move?"

Now that was more like the Booker she knew and loved. "Just the bedroom furniture. I already moved the small stuff and my clothes." She turned to meander down the hallway and

Booker followed. Closely. She could practically feel him breathing on her neck. Neil Diamond's Christmas album played softly in the background, barely drowning out the drumming of her heartbeat.

Today, even Neil hadn't been able to lift her spirits.

As they passed the kitchen, they walked beneath a sprig of mistletoe hung from a silver ribbon. Because she was a single woman without a steady date—without any date really—Frances had put it up as a decoration, not for any practical use. She paid it little mind as she started under it, until Booker caught her by the upper arm.

Turning, she said, "What?"

Gently, he drew her all the way around to face him. He looked first into her eyes, letting her see the curious heat in his, then he looked at her mouth. His voice dropped. "This."

In the next instant, Frances found herself hauled up against his hard chest while his hands framed her face.

Startled, she thought, *He's going to kiss me.*

Just as quickly, she discounted that absurd notion. Booker was a friend, nothing more. He was involved with Judith. He didn't see her as a—

His mouth touched hers.

She went utterly still outside, but inside things were happening. Like her heart hitting her rib cage and her stomach fluttering and her blood taking off in a wild race through her system . . .

"Frances?" He whispered her name against her mouth.

Dazed, her eyes flickered open. "Hmm?"

Booker held her face tipped up, brushed her jaw with his thumbs, and kissed her again. It was a gentle, closed-mouth kiss, but there was nothing platonic about it. His mouth was warm, soft, moving carefully over hers. His tongue traced the seam of her lips with such enticing effect that her toes curled and her hands lifted to his hard shoulders. Booker groaned, tightened his hold—and Frances came back to her senses.

"*Booker.*" She shoved him away, suffused with indignation and hurt and an awful yearning. "What do you think you're doing?"

Because she was nearly as tall, her push had thrown him off-balance. He caught himself, grinned at her, and said, "Something I've been thinking about doing for a long time."

Frances touched her mouth, equally doubting and flustered. She could still taste him. "You have?"

"Yeah. I have." He closed the space between them again. Frances inhaled the clean scent of his aftershave and the headier scent of his body. She could practically feel the heat in his unwavering gaze. He touched her chin, tipped up her face, and asked, "Haven't you, Frances? Ever?"

Chapter Two

Frances swallowed hard. Think of him? Of course, she had. There were nights when she couldn't sleep at all, fantasizing about Booker, about kissing him and touching him, feeling his weight on top of her, naked flesh to naked flesh. But all she did was fantasize because he was already with someone else and she would never, ever want to be blamed for breaking up a couple.

She couldn't lie to him, but she wouldn't be a party to him cheating either. "Yes, I have."

His expression tightened, his voice went deep. "Tell me."

God, he was potent in seduce-mode. "No. Because I'm not going to do anything about it."

"Wanna bet?"

Oh, the wicked way he murmured that. "Booker Dean, have you forgotten that you're already involved? Have you forgotten about *Judith?*" Damn, she hadn't meant to sneer the woman's name. It wasn't Judith's fault that Booker had fallen in love with her long before Frances had even moved into his apartment complex. She scowled. "You know you don't really want to do this."

"Oh, I want to all right." He kept inching toward her, forcing her to back up. "You probably have no idea of all the things I want to do to you."

Her mouth fell open, then snapped shut. "Let me rephrase that. I won't let you do them."

He reached out and brushed her cheek with the back of his knuckles. His voice was soft, mesmerizing. "Even though Judith and I aren't together anymore?"

"You aren't . . ." Her eyes narrowed. "Since when?"

With a load of satisfaction, Booker said, "About twenty minutes ago."

Forget indignation. Frances was outraged. She stopped retreating and took a stand. Through stiffened lips, she said, "Judith breaks up with you twenty minutes ago and so you come tripping over here expecting . . . what? You want me to comfort you, Booker? Is that it? You want to use me to forget about her?"

Booker looked momentarily nonplussed, then annoyed. "No, damn it. That's just dumb. Besides, she didn't break up with me."

That surprised Frances. "You're the one who broke things off?"

He worked his jaw. "Well, not yet. Not officially. But see . . ."

Frances threw up her arms. "I don't believe this. Go home, Booker." She turned and stomped down the hall to her bedroom. *Not officially,* she mimicked in her mind. Damn. She hit a pillow, but it didn't help. She'd wanted Booker too long to play games like this.

Conflicting emotions wreaked havoc with her heart. She'd dreamed of Booker seeing her as more than a friend, but never would she allow him to use her to get over another woman.

She started to hit the pillow again, then Booker slipped his arms around her from behind. All along the length of her back, she felt him, hot, hard, most definitely male. Because he held a physical job, Booker's strength was evidenced in lean, hard muscles. When Frances started to jolt away, he carefully restrained her, gathering her close against his body, enfolding her in that delicious scent. "Just hold on and let me explain."

She'd melt if she stayed pressed to him like this. In a rasp, she whispered, "Let go."

"No."

His refusal gave her pause, then renewed her temper. She'd never known Booker to be a dominating-type man. "What do you mean no? I said to let me go."

Instead, he immobilized her by kissing the side of her neck. Stunned, Frances registered the heat and firmness of his mouth, the soft touch of his damp tongue—and she registered his smile. "Honest to God, Frannie, you make me nuts. You've been making me nuts for a while now." His arms tightened in a bear hug and he rocked her side to side.

Holding herself stiff against the urge to relax in his embrace, Frances said, "Well it wasn't on purpose."

"I know," he soothed. "You can't help it."

"Booker—"

He interrupted her warning with another soft smooch, this one behind her ear. That small kiss, accompanied with the sigh of his breath, had her breathing accelerating and her temperature on the rise. She shivered.

"There, you see? You do it without even trying."

"Do . . . what?"

"Make me crazy." He pressed his nose into her hair. "With the way you smell—"

Smell? She tried for sarcasm to save her. "You mean like paint thinner and clay?"

"And woman and sex and *you*, Frannie Kennedy. I love how you smell." He took another deep breath, then growled to show his sincerity. "And the way you dress."

Now she rolled her eyes. "In paint-stained work clothes? C'mon Booker." Since they couldn't be more than friends, she'd made a point of *not* primping with him. In the last few weeks, he'd started coming over more often, staying longer when he did, and she'd come to appreciate how nice it was to be totally herself with someone. She could forget makeup and uncomfortably stylish clothes. She could laugh out loud without worrying if he found her inelegant. She could blow her nose when she had a cold or sniffle and cry at sad movies. She could cheer as loud as any guy when her favorite football team won, and she could even share a few dirty jokes with him without blushing.

Now he wanted to throw a kink in the works.

Booker's hands opened over her middle. He had large hands, rough from working in his lumberyard and doing custom millwork. With his fingers splayed, he was only a millimeter from her breasts with one hand, and closer than that to her left hipbone with the other.

Anticipation held her in thrall. Would he touch her? Would she let him?

His warm breath brushed her ear. "In soft loose smocks that tease because they hide your breasts, making my imagination go wild."

She didn't know Booker had ever noticed her breasts. They certainly weren't big enough to automatically draw attention.

". . . and snug leggings that make your ass look great."

Her *ass*? She tried to twist to see him, but he wouldn't let her.

". . . and thick socks that look so cute on your feet."

Being almost as tall as him meant her feet were proportionate—and not in the least cute. "Now you're just being ridiculous."

"Frannie, Frannie, Frannie. You'd be amazed at what appears sexual to the male mind, especially when it's been deprived. Like the funny way you always pin up your hair." He teased a twisted lock with his nose. "It's sort of sloppy and casual, but I can see your nape and those baby-fine curls there and it makes me horny as hell." To emphasize that, he took a gentle love bite at the side of her throat.

Frances swallowed down a gasp, both of shock and sexual spark. Against her behind, she felt the start of an impressive erection. She gave a small, nearly silent moan. It took all her willpower not to nestle up closer to that purely male reaction— *to her.*

But willpower was something she'd cultivated since moving next door to Booker Dean. When she'd first met him, she'd panicked because he was so appealing and she'd been a complete wreck, a typical state for her when she worked, and she worked almost all the time. But when she'd realized he was already taken and so off-limits, she'd given up and been herself and found a wonderful friendship that no matter how she tried wasn't quite enough.

It still wasn't enough, but she'd be damned before she got him on the rebound.

"So," she said, forcing the word out while closing her hands around his wrists to ensure he wouldn't move them up or down. "You're not officially over with Judith, but you expect me to just say, 'Hey, okay, let's go to bed'?"

He shuddered against her, asking roughly, "Would you?"

"No." She again started to lunge away but Booker held on and they stumbled into the wall.

"If you'll just settle down and listen, I'll explain." Cautiously, he turned her around so she faced him. Then, before she could protest, he looked at her mouth, appeared drawn there and he started kissing her again, light, teasing kisses. "I swear, Frannie, you have the sexiest mouth."

"In about two seconds, I'm going to unman you with my knee." He released her and stepped back so quickly, she almost smiled. "Now, if you insist, you can explain while you help me move my stuff." If he kept his hands busy moving her furniture, he couldn't have them busy feeling her up, and she wouldn't have to worry about resisting him.

He followed her to the bedroom, reacting to her antagonism with inexhaustible good humor. "Sure thing, Frannie." Muscles flexed and his shoulders strained when he hefted a nightstand high and started out the door with it. "Hey, do you realize your room will be right next to mine now?"

Frances froze in the process of lifting a plant. Good God, he was right. Only a thin apartment wall would separate them now. He came back into the room, saw her stunned expression, and clicked his tongue. "What are you thinking, Frances Kennedy? Can I trust you not to put your ear to the wall? Will you drill a hole and peek at me at night? I sleep naked you know."

Heat pulsed in her cheeks. "Booker . . ."

"In fact, if you actually want a peek, I'd be more than happy to—" He reached for the snap on his jeans.

Frances shoved the plant into his arms. "I was just wondering if I'd have to listen to you and Judith."

He chided her with a look. "Nope. I told you,

that's over. Actually, it's been over for a month. I just wasn't sure how to finish it off."

She desperately wanted to believe that. "So what changed?"

With great relish, he confided, "She wants Axel."

"She *what?*"

Booker laughed. "Don't sound so shocked. I haven't met too many women who don't want Axel."

"Well, I certainly don't." Axel was a nice enough guy, and she could see why he'd be popular with the females. But it was this particular brother who pushed all her buttons. Not Axel. Not any other man.

"I'm really glad to hear that. He can have Judith, but I don't want him to even look at you funny."

Like a zombie, Frances moved to the end of her mattress and helped Booker lift it. Her thoughts were churning this way and that. "You don't seem upset that she might want your brother."

"No 'might' to it, and no, as I told Axel, I'm relieved." He winked at Frances. "Leaves me free and clear for other . . . pursuits."

Frances ignored that bit of nonsense for now. "Did Judith tell you she wanted Axel?"

"No." Booker wrestled his end of the mattress into the other room. "From my understanding, she just caught Axel alone and tried to molest him."

Frances snorted. "Yeah right. Like Axel ever needs to be coerced."

Booker paused to give her a long look around the side of the mattress. "He's my brother, honey. Whatever else he might be, he's loyal to family."

Somewhat chastened, Frances dropped her end of the mattress. "Meaning he wouldn't go behind your back with Judith?"

"That's right. She came on to him, he turned her down, but felt he had to let me know. Rightfully so because what man wants to tie himself to a woman who's after his brother?"

"Only an idiot."

"And I'm sure we'll both agree I'm not an idiot." He didn't wait for her agreement at all. "But as it turns out, I'm pleased to have the perfect opportunity to end things." He, too, let his end of the mattress rest on the floor. "I'd been working on that anyway."

Frances bit her lip and tried not to sound too hopeful. "You have?"

"Yeah, I have. Only I'm a nice guy and I didn't want to hurt her." His voice lowered. "We haven't been . . . close for a month anyway."

It had been about a month that he'd been coming around more often, staying longer, teasing her more. But did he mean he hadn't slept with Judith in a month? Her brows drew down in disbelief.

"Now Frannie, don't look at me like that. Have I ever lied to you?"

"No. But you've never acted interested either."

He sighed, lifted the mattress again and dragged it the rest of the way into the room. Frances thought he was going to let the subject drop until he said, "I've always been attracted to you, Frannie. From the first time I saw you, I knew I wanted you."

She swallowed hard, frowned, then turned away. Booker followed her back into the bedroom where they tackled the bedsprings next. Unable to keep it in, she finally grumbled, "You hid it well."

He grinned. "Really? Maybe I should have been an actor." They both strained to get the cumbersome bedsprings through the doorway. Once it was in place with the mattress, Booker dusted off his hands. "I must be more accomplished than I realized. I mean, I know I didn't come right out and tell you, but if all the attention didn't clue you in, then I thought for sure the occasional boner would be a giveaway."

Frances silently cursed herself for blushing again. She retreated back to her room to dismantle the bed frame.

Booker knelt beside her. "Frances?"

"I never noticed."

"Never noticed what?"

Keeping her attention on the task at hand, she blindly gestured toward his lap and gave a whopper of a lie. "Any . . . boners."

Booker clutched his heart theatrically and toppled back on his rear. "God, I'm wounded. You really know how to damage the old male vanity, hon."

Laughing, Frances lifted one half of the frame and stood. Truth was, she'd noticed a few erections here and there, but had always discounted them as some strange male phenomenon. Guys got hard for the most ridiculous reasons.

Booker came to his feet to face her. Losing his smile, he stared at her with beguiling seriousness and seductive charm. "How about now?"

"Now?"

Without looking away from her eyes, he took her wrist and carried her hand to his fly where a thick ridge had risen beneath his denims. The second her fingers touched him, he caught his breath and his voice went hoarse. "Can you notice this one?"

A rush of giddiness nearly took Frances's knees out from under her. He was long, thick, and hard . . . how could she not notice? She thought of him naked, thought of him pressing inside her, filling her up, and her fingers curled tight around him. Booker's eyes closed and she heard the roughness of his breathing.

Filled with curiosity, she traced his length upward, then back down again, measuring him, teasing herself. Booker locked his jaw. "Keep that up and I'm going to lose it."

She barely heard his words. Lifting her other hand, she covered him completely, stroking, squeezing, reaching lower to feel the heavy weight of his testicles. His teeth clenched. "Frances, I've wanted you too long to have any patience. Add that to month-long celibacy, and I'm working on a hair trigger here."

So, it really had been a month? That meant something, didn't it?

He stood rigid before her, letting her do as she pleased. Or rather, as she dared. She wanted to push him to the floor and strip him naked, but everything had happened too quickly . . .

Releasing him, she stepped back. It took him a moment, but Booker finally got his eyes open. He looked in pain. He looked ready to jump her bones. Suggestively, he said, "Why don't we finish putting the bed together?"

"All right."

His eyes flared at her agreement.

Damn it, she hated her conscience sometimes. "But Booker, I can't . . . we can't, do anything until you've officially broken things off with Judith. You said you're a nice guy. Well, I'm a nice woman. And like your brother, I want no part of poaching."

Booker frowned. "Speaking with her is just a formality at this point."

"It's a formality I'll have to insist on." In the darkest part of her soul, Frances was afraid that Judith would beg him not to leave her, and he'd agree. She knew it was wrong to hope things would be over between them, especially if Judith would be hurt. But she wished it just the same.

Booker hesitated a long moment before agreeing. "All right. Let's get done here and I'll go call her. But it won't matter, Frannie, not to me."

Hoping that was true, Frances nodded. They spent the next hour setting up her bedroom. Booker even helped her remake the bed, then rearrange everything in her new studio so that the job was complete. The busy work afforded Frances a little time to think about the new turn of events.

When they'd finished and the last item was in

place, Booker caught both her hands and bent to kiss her. "If Judith is home, I could be back here in no time."

Booker Dean was more temptation than any woman should have to endure. Regretfully, Frances shook her head. "Booker, I need some time to adjust to this. You can't just expect me to take it all in stride."

"Do you want me, Frances?"

"Yes." She didn't mind admitting that much. "I have for a long time."

His triumphant smile was sexy and pure male.

"But I still need some time to think things through."

"How much time?"

"I don't know. At least until tomorrow."

Disappointment showed in the drawing of his brows, the darkening of his eyes. "Tomorrow, huh?"

Unable to continue meeting his gaze, Frances looked down at her feet. "You need time to think about this too, you know. You could still change your mind. You might be here on the rebound or because you want validation because Judith tried to cheat on you." Frances shrugged, feeling a little helpless, caught between wanting to say *yes* and having enough common sense to say *not yet.* "I want you, but I don't want to be used and I don't want regrets and even more than that, I don't want things to get weird between us if we do this, and then tomorrow or the next day or a month from now, you're back with Judith."

Booker said nothing to all that, and Frances

had the feeling he waited for her to look at him. Finally she did and got trapped in the mesmerizing intensity of his dark gaze. She had the bed at her back, Booker in front of her, and a whole lot of desire crackling in the air between them.

One side of Booker's mouth tipped in a sensual smile, then he stepped up against her and toppled her onto the mattress. Before she could catch her breath, he came down over her. His solid chest crushed her breasts, his hard abdomen pressed into her stomach. Like a tidal wave, desire rolled through her.

Booker cupped her face, kissed her nose, her forehead, her chin. "I don't want Judith. I haven't wanted Judith since I got to know you. But I'll wait. I'll give you some time. And while you're thinking things over, Frances, think about this."

His earlier kisses had been teasing, tentative. This one scorched her.

Using his thumbs, he nudged her chin down so her lips parted. He sank his tongue in, leisurely exploring while giving her that full-body contact she'd craved for so long.

Her hands gripped his shoulders, holding on. His hips moved in a carnal press and retreat, mimicking how he'd take her if only she'd say yes. Frances moaned, then moaned again when his fingers found her breast, gently cuddled her, traced her nipple—and then he was gone.

It wasn't easy, but she got her eyes open to see Booker standing between her legs at the side of the bed. He stared down at her, his face flushed, his chest heaving, his dark gaze fierce.

Frances pushed up on one elbow. "Booker?"

"If I don't go now, I won't go at all. But I want more than just a quick tumble, Frannie. You'll figure that out on your own, without me pushing you. So . . . good night." He took one step back from the bed. "Think about me tonight. And try trusting me just a little."

She watched him leave the room, then dropped back down to the mattress with a long groan. Good gracious, Booker on the make was even more exciting than she'd ever imagined. And if he was like this when she said no, how tantalizing would he be when she finally said yes?

Chapter Three

No way was she going to be able to sleep. It was midnight, but her body hummed and her mind was in turmoil. Had he called Judith yet? What had happened?

Frances punched the pillow, moaned in frustration, and rolled to her side. She'd asked for tonight to think. But all she could think about was whether he'd called Judith, what might have happened, if it was really over. Why didn't he call and tell her?

She moaned again. When she saw him tomorrow, she'd . . .

"Frances?"

She froze at the muffled call of her name. Eyes wide in the dark, she peered around but saw nothing. No one.

A knock sounded on the wall right behind her head. "C'mon Frannie. I hear you in there." The squeak of his bed resonated through the wall.

Frances jerked upright. "Booker?"

"Of course, it's Booker. I told you we'd be sleeping right next to each other." Silence, then: "Why did you moan?" And sounding a little wishful: "Thinking of me?"

"Yes."

Throbbing silence. "What *are* you doing over there, Frannie?"

The way he said that, she knew exactly what *he* thought she was doing. She punched the wall, heard him curse softly, and smiled. "Get your mind out of the gutter, you pervert. I was beating up my pillow."

"How come?"

Because you made me all hot and bothered and then walked away. "Because I can't sleep."

"And? You can't sleep because . . . ?"

Through her teeth, Frances snarled, "Because I'm wondering if you spoke with Judith and how it went, but you didn't bother to call and tell me."

"Oh."

A few seconds later, her phone pealed loudly, giving Frances a horrible start. She stared toward the nightstand in the dark, then groped across the bed until she found it. She lifted the receiver. "Hello?"

"I called her."

Her fingers curled tightly. "And?"

There was a definite shrug in Booker's tone. "Axel answered."

"*Axel* answered?" Frances collapsed back against the headboard. Man, Booker's brother hadn't wasted any time. Of course, where women were concerned, he seldom did.

But Booker didn't seem perturbed by his brother's rush into his ex's bed. "Yeah. He sounded winded, too, so I'm thinking I interrupted things."

Her eyes flared wide again. "You interrupted things?"

Laughing, Booker asked, "Are you going to repeat everything I say?"

"Maybe." She couldn't believe how cavalier he was about the whole thing.

"I want you."

Frances gripped the phone, swallowed hard.

"Not going to repeat that, huh?" He sighed, very put out. "Anyway, Axel put Judith on the line, she apologized, said she was drunk. Then I heard Axel grousing at her and pretty soon, she was giggling, then panting. I don't know what he did to her, but she liked it because she finally admitted that she'd been thinking about Axel for a long time, and because of that, she knew she wasn't ready to settle down."

"Um . . . wow." Frances cleared her throat. "I don't know what to say."

"I say all's well that ends well. At least with those two. Now concerning you." His voice dropped. "I need your trust, Frannie."

Knowing she'd never get to sleep now, Frances

flipped on the lamp and got out of bed. A peek out the darkened window showed drifting snow and ice crystals covering every surface. It looked magical, perfectly picturesque for Christmastime, and perfect to help clear her mind.

With the phone caught between her shoulder and ear, she pulled on thickly lined nylon jogging pants. "It's not a matter of trust, Booker. You've just done a hundred-and-eighty turn, and we both need time to adjust."

"What are you doing?" He sounded suspicious.

"Nothing." She sat on the bed to pull on two pairs of socks and her all-weather running shoes.

"Frances Kennedy, are you getting dressed?"

A new alertness had entered his tone, so she hesitated before finally saying in a small voice, "Yes."

The phone clicked in her ear. Well. In a huff, Frances put the phone back in the cradle and stood. Over her T-shirt, she layered on a thermal shirt and finally a sweatshirt. After wrapping a muffler around her throat, pulling a wool hat low over her ears and grabbing up her mittens, she headed for the apartment door.

She opened it only to find Booker standing there in hastily donned jeans and nothing else. He pushed his way in, forcing her back inside.

"Oh no, you don't." He flattened himself against the closed door, arms spread, naked feet braced apart, blocking her from leaving. The sparse sprinkling of dark hair over his chest drew Frances's attention. She'd seen his bare chest before, but always with the awareness that she couldn't, shouldn't stare. Now she could. And she did.

His chest hair was crisp, spreading from nipple to nipple, and a line of silkier hair trailed happily from his chest down his abdomen. Fascinated, she visually traced it as it twirled around a tight navel, then dipped beneath his unsnapped jeans. Lord have mercy.

It wasn't easy, but Frances got her attention back on his face—and caught his indulgent look of satisfaction. "What are you doing here, Booker?" *Besides looking like sin personified.*

"Supplying some common sense, apparently." Vibrating tension brought him away from the door until he stood nose to nose with Frances. "It's too cold, too late and way too damn dark to be out running around by yourself."

"Wanna go with me?" She wouldn't mind the company.

"Hell no." He shivered for emphasis and began unwinding her muffler. "We'd both end up with pneumonia."

"I can't sleep. Running helps me relax."

Eyes twinkling, he opened his mouth and Frances, knowing good and well what his alternate suggestion would be, snapped, "No, don't say it, Booker. I told you I wanted time and damn it, I'll get time."

His grin sent a curl of heat through her stomach. He whipped off her hat, kissed her nose. "Okay. Then let's make cookies." Eyebrows bobbing, he added in a growl, "I *love* your cookies."

Well, that was nothing less than the truth. She'd already made him several batches of frosted Christmas cookies and they never lasted him long. She supposed baking would be as distracting as running. "All right. But you have to help."

Using both hands, he pushed his bed-rumpled hair away from his face. "My pleasure. Lead the way."

This time she dodged the mistletoe as she headed to the kitchen, making Booker laugh. She pulled out flour and sugar, eggs and other ingredients, and he got her big glass bowls off the top shelf.

"You know," Booker said thoughtfully, "while you're getting used to the idea, I could detail all the benefits of a more intimate relationship between us."

Frances bit back a moan. The intimate benefits were already more than apparent to her. She didn't need them detailed. Keeping her back to him and carefully measuring in vanilla, she said, "I have a good imagination, Booker. I don't need any help."

"But I want to tell you." He came up behind her, caught her hips in his hands and kissed her ear. "It occurred to me that there may be nuances involved that you haven't considered."

Her right hand held an egg suspended over a bowl. "Yeah? Like what?" She leaned into him, tilted her head to give him better advantage, and sighed when his kisses trailed to her throat. She'd dated plenty of times, even semiseriously once or twice, but she'd never known the side of her neck was that sensitive.

Then again, maybe it was just Booker. Everywhere he touched her made her senses riot.

She knew she should resist him, but it just wasn't possible.

"Like tonight," he whispered huskily. "When you're restless, I'll be right there to help." He smiled against her throat. "But if you insist on jogging at night, I can go with you. Or we can make more cookies."

"Sounds . . . interesting." Truth was, she couldn't clear her thoughts long enough to decide what made sense and what didn't. Not with Booker touching her.

"You wouldn't have to worry about finding a date."

"I never worry about that anyway."

The squeeze he gave her nearly took her breath away. "I know. How come you never go out much?"

Because she loved him and he'd been with Judith. "I dated a lot before I moved here. But since then, I've had one job after another. Especially with the holidays." Recently, with her growing popularity, every small gallery around had wanted to put on a show with her work.

Booker stepped away from her, enabling her to draw a deep, fortifying breath. "That's another thing," he said. "When you're working nonstop the way you do sometimes, I can help with your dinner and chores."

Slowly, Frances turned to face him. What he suggested sounded a whole lot more involved than an affair. Because everything was so new, she didn't have the nerve to ask him to spell out his intentions. Instead, she said, "I can take care of myself."

His expression warmed with tenderness. "You're the strongest woman I know. I admire you a lot, Frannie."

He admired her.

"You're also smart and funny, and I love how I can be myself with you."

He'd said the *L* word, and it nearly stopped her heart. She watched him with wide eyes and growing tension.

"But Frannie, wouldn't it be nice to have someone to cuddle with at night? Wouldn't it be nice to go Christmas shopping together for gifts? To wake up Christmas morning and share all the magic and fun?"

It felt like her tongue had stuck to the roof of her mouth. He implied that he wanted to . . . move in?

"I'd like you to meet my folks. They're great. You can't judge them by Axel," he teased. "He's the black sheep of the family. Were you planning to go home on Christmas?"

He ran that all together too quickly, leaving her dazed. "Christmas Eve," she murmured, still trying to mentally catch up with him.

"Great. Then I could go there with you and we could hit my folk's place Christmas morning. Gramps and Gramma will be there. Hell, they're ninety now, but still have a wicked sense of humor. There'll be some aunts and uncles, too.

Do you have big get-togethers? How many of your relatives will I get to meet?"

Her head spun. She almost dropped the stupid egg but caught herself in time. Turning back to the large bowl, she began adding ingredients. "There's, uh, about twenty of us. Lots of kids. My two sisters are already married."

"I bet they all tease you about being single."

Her chin lifted. "Actually, they consider me the strange artsy one in the bunch. They never know quite what to expect from me." For certain, they wouldn't expect Booker.

"Strange? Really?" He said it with amusement.

"And why not? Look how different I am from Judith."

"Yeah." She felt his gaze tracking over her body, pausing in prime places until she almost squirmed. "You're different all right."

Just what the hell did he mean by that? Flustered, she dumped in too much sugar. "Set the oven on 350."

"Yes, ma'am." He took care of that before leaning beside her against the counter. Without a shirt and his jeans undone, he proved a mighty distraction. "Now, about these differences."

Frances stirred the batter with single-minded ferocity. "Judith is beautiful."

With a snort, Booker leaned around to see her face. "You're an artist, Frannie. You know you're easy on the eyes."

"I know I'm not a hag," she specified. "But I am too thin and probably too tall."

"You're damn near the same height as me."

"Exactly. And judging by Judith, you like women who are elegant. Judith always had her hair just right, her makeup perfect and her nails freshly painted."

Indulgently, Booker tucked her hair behind her ear. "And the only paint I see on you is often on your nose."

Rolling her eyes, Frances said, "Or under my nails, rather than on them." She hesitated a moment, unsure how many comparisons she wanted to make. "Judith has bigger boobs, too."

His grin came and went quickly. "She's got a nice rack on her, true. But Frannie?" When she glanced up at him, he said, "She's not you." He stroked the side of her throat. "You make me laugh, almost as much as you make me hot. I enjoy being with you, talking to you. I knew things were over with Judith when I decided I'd rather watch football with you than sleep with her."

Frances paused in her stirring. "Has it really been a month?"

"At least. It feels longer because I've wanted you more every damn day." When she stood there, just staring at him, he gently nudged her aside and began scooping the cookie dough into the press he'd taken from her cabinet. "I should have realized Judith felt the same when she didn't protest my lack of interest. But everyone kept talking about us being an item, hinting that we should get married. And it was the holidays, a bad time to dump someone. And so, like an idiot, I tried to figure out a way to end it without causing a big scene—so I could be with you."

He began turning the crank on the old press and a tree-shaped cookie appeared on the baking sheet. "You," he told her with a sideways glance of accusation, "kept treating me like some asexual buddy."

Frances gasped in affront. "That's how *you* treated *me*."

"Not by choice. I just wanted to make sure I didn't scare you off until I could tell you how I really felt."

The baking sheet now held two dozen small trees. Frances took it from him, opened the oven and bent at the waist to slide it in.

"Oh, sweetheart," he said from right behind her, "you don't know what you're advertising there."

Frances glanced around to see him staring at her behind. She jerked upright, her face flushed from his attention and the heat that wafted from the oven.

Booker reached out, caught her elbow and dragged her close. "You're too warm." So saying, he caught the hem of her sweatshirt and pulled it up and over her head. "Damn, how many layers are you wearing?"

"Enough to jog outside without freezing."

"Well, maybe you can be an early present and I'll just keep unwrapping you." He removed her thermal shirt too, leaving her in an oversized blue T-shirt and gray nylon jogging pants. He stared at her breasts and said, "I don't suppose you'd want to do a little making out? We could sort of ease into things with a lot of kissing, maybe a little petting. Then tomorrow when you've made up your mind—"

Frances threw her arms around his neck. "Yes."

Chapter Four

Surprised by her sudden acquiescence, Booker lifted her to the countertop and moved her knees apart to stand between them. Frances's eyes widened, but he didn't give her time to change her mind. He kissed her.

God, he'd never get used to her taste, her softness. The T-shirt hugged her small breasts, showing the strained outline of her puckered nipples. He slid his hands down her sides, enthralled by her narrow waist, the firmness of her supple muscles. As a runner, she stayed toned and trim. He couldn't wait to feel her legs around him, squeezing him tight.

But she wanted a day to think about it, so by God, he'd give her a day. Tonight he'd only tease, show her what they could have together in an effort to hedge his bets. It was a ruthless move, but then, he'd wanted her too damn long to play fair.

He took her mouth in a long drugging kiss, meant to distract her while he slipped his hands beneath her shirt. She felt warm and firm and soft and he knew he'd bust his jeans if he prolonged this too long. The silky skin of her back drew him first. She was so slight of build, so narrow that with his fingers spread, he could span her width. He rubbed back down her sides, then up to her breasts, just under them, not touching her yet despite the urge to weigh her in his palms, to learn her.

"Booker . . ." she groaned, and the way she said his name pushed him that much closer to the edge.

Using his thumbs, he stroked her nipples, felt them stiffen, and he couldn't take it. He leaned back, pulled the shirt up to bare her and inhaled sharply at the sight of her.

"Frannie." He could feel her hesitancy. Her breasts were small, perfectly shaped with dark pink nipples. He bent to take one puckered nipple into his mouth, drawing gently, flicking with his tongue.

Her reaction was electric. She stiffened, lacing her fingers tight into his hair, pulling him closer. Her legs opened wider around him and Booker used one arm to pull her to the very edge of the counter, in direct contact with his hips.

Her groan was long and gratifying.

Earlier, he'd been on the ragged edge, damn

near ready to come in his pants. But now he had her where he wanted her. Almost. Naked would be better, but he'd make do.

"I'm going to make you come, Frannie."

Her eyes snapped open and she stiffened, but Booker didn't let her gather her wits enough to retreat. Carefully, he laid her back on the counter, kissing her deeply again until she sighed and clung to him. Stroking her, he smoothed his hand over her shoulder, down her side, and to her hip. The elastic waistband of her jogging pants proved accommodating.

Her stomach sucked in and she gasped.

"Shhh . . ." he told her, then groaned when he found her panties damp. "God, I've dreamed of touching you like this."

He heard her fast shallow breaths and lifted his head. Eyes wide, she stared at the ceiling. Her face was warm, her breasts rising and falling as she panted, her nipples achingly tight.

Booker gently pushed one finger inside her, gritting his teeth against the instant clasp of her body. Her lips parted on a deep inhalation. "How's that feel?" he asked her, slipping his finger in and out, his voice so low and hoarse he barely recognized himself.

Rather than answer, her neck arched and her eyes closed. With his heart slamming hard enough to shake his body, Booker went back to her breasts—at the same time working in a second finger. She was tight, but so wet and hot he knew she would enjoy the slight stretch of ultra-sensitive flesh.

Her legs opened wider.

Nipping gently with his lips, he teased her nipple. He circled with his tongue, held her with his teeth and tugged until she cried out, rolling her hips against his hand, bathing his fingers in slick moisture. He found her clitoris with his thumb, pressed, and then let her set her pace.

"Booker," she whispered, then again, a little louder, a little more shrill, *"Booker."*

God, yes, he thought, thrilled with her response. He held her closer to still her movements. While thrusting his fingers harder, faster, he sucked strongly at her nipple. In a sudden rush of sensation, she climaxed, her body bowing on the countertop, her cries loud and sweet. Booker had to fight back his own orgasm so he didn't embarrass himself by coming in his pants.

Slowly, Frannie subsided, her body going limp by small degrees. She'd managed to knock the clip out of her hair and it tumbled around her face, a little tangled, a little sweaty. Booker leaned over her, smiling, feeling pretty damn good except for a straining, painful erection.

He touched her lax mouth, brushed a pale blond lock away from her forehead. "I love you, Frannie."

Her eyes snapped open—and the oven dinged.

Good timing, Booker decided. He knew he could take her now and all her protestations wouldn't mean a thing. She was soft, limp, open to him in body and emotions. Her gently parted lips told him so. The flush of her skin told him so. Her heavy, unfocused eyes told him so.

But he'd promised her and because he loved her, because he wanted her for the rest of his life, not just tonight, he slid his arms under her shoulders and lifted her off the counter. She was unsteady on her feet, weaving until he steadied her.

Her T-shirt fell into place. He helped readjust her displaced jogging pants. After a teasing flick on her nose, he said, "The cookies will burn," and went to fetch a potholder to remove the tray from the oven. The air filled with the humid scents of sugary cookies, and the more subtle scent of aroused woman.

When he turned to face Frances again, she hadn't moved. She was still staring at him, mute, but also drowsy with satisfaction.

Booker sighed. "I'm going to go now. If I don't, you won't get that time you need to think about things."

That brought her around, her eyes blinking and her shoulders straightening. "You need time to think too, to make sure—"

"No." He reached out and brushed one fingertip over her left breast, making her shudder anew. "I know what I want."

"You mean right now?" She swallowed. "Or tomorrow?"

Smiling, Booker told her, "I already got what I wanted right now. Thank you."

She blinked rapidly again. "You're welcome."

"Tomorrow I'd love to have you naked, so I can really love you properly. So I can come with you. Inside you."

She rolled her lips in on a soft moan.

"After that," he said, looking at her directly, making sure she understood, "I want *everything*. Every day, every night, the rest of our lives."

She drew a shuddering breath, opened her mouth to speak, and Booker put a finger to her lips. "No, honey. Just do your thinking, okay? We'll talk in the morning."

"But—"

"Can you sleep now? I don't have to worry about you slipping outside?"

"I can sleep."

She already looked halfway there, amusing him and blunting the lust with tenderness. He cupped her jaw. "I love you, Frannie," he stated again, then he went to her door and walked out.

Frances woke slowly, a smile on her mouth. He loved her. Her Christmas wishes had come true. Feeling energized despite the fact she'd only had a few hours sleep, she threw off the covers and went to the window. More snow had fallen, blanketing the world in a dazzling display of silver and white. It was so awe-inspiring it took her breath away.

A tap sounded on her bedroom wall. "G'morning, beautiful."

Almost dancing in her happiness, Frances dashed back to the bed and laid her hand on the wall. "Good morning, Booker."

"I miss you."

She hugged herself in giddy pleasure. "It hasn't been that long. Why are you up?"

"Because a sexy broad turned me inside out last night, then sent me to my lonely bed. Oh wait. Do you mean why am I out of bed?"

She chuckled. "Booker Dean, you know exactly what I meant." He *had* gone home alone, all because he was so considerate and wonderful . . . and he said he loved her. She wanted to stand up and sing.

"Well, as to that, I was hoping that same sexy broad would have something special to say to me today. I've been laying here just waiting."

Frances fell back on the mattress, arms wide, heart full. Oh, she had things to say to him. Lots and lots of things. What he'd done to her last night, how he'd made her feel . . .

She sat back up and spoke close to the wall. "She just might." Booker had said today he wanted her naked, then he wanted her for the rest of their lives. She badly wanted to give him whatever he wanted. Struck with sudden, very daring inspiration, Frances glanced at the clock. She bit her lip, hesitated, then forced herself to say, "I'll need an hour, okay?"

"Right. One hour. But keep in mind I'll be holding my breath." He tapped on the wall, and Frances knew he'd left the room. She jumped up and dashed into the shower. This was going to be the most magical Christmas ever—one that would start her on a new life with the man she loved.

* * *

Booker got out of the shower at the sound of knocking on his door. Frances? Damn, he hoped so. He pulled a towel around his hips and went to greet her.

Unfortunately, it was Axel and Cary, not Frances. They sported a box of doughnuts, beard-shadowed cheeks, and red-rimmed eyes.

"Morning, Booker," Axel said as he walked in, then nudged the door shut behind him. "Did you lock me out on purpose?"

Booker headed to his bedroom to dress. "It's only seven in the morning. I always lock my door at night when I sleep."

Cary said, "See? It wasn't personal." Then to Booker, "I'm going to put on coffee."

Booker emerged wearing jeans and carrying a shirt and sneakers. "No. Your coffee sucks. I'll get it." Feeling a touch of déjà vu, Booker pulled his shirt over his head, pushed his feet into his sneakers, and began coffee preparations. "All right. Why the early-morning visit?"

Cary grinned. "You are so damn suspicious, Booker. Hell, we're just heading home after pulling an all-nighter."

"Together?"

"No." Axel fished out a fat jelly doughnut and took a large bite. "We hooked up for breakfast, then decided you might want doughnuts, too."

"You were with Judith all night?"

Axel paused in the middle of chewing. "Is that okay?"

"I keep telling you that it is. Just don't ever try it with Frannie. I don't even want you looking at her. Got it?"

"I'll wear blinders when the girl is around."

"See that you do." He finished the coffee. "I'm kind of amazed at your speed with Judith, though."

Grinning, Axel said, "Yeah, well, she's been converted."

"Axel-fied?" Cary asked.

"Exactly. And who can think of marriage when I'm having so much fun being single?"

Booker's front door opened again and Frances called softly, "Booker?"

Knowing he grinned like a sap and not caring in the least, Booker saluted his brother and Cary. "I'll be right back." He would allow his brother one cup of coffee, and then he'd oust him for some alone-time with Frannie.

She stood uncertainly inside his door, her bare feet shifting on his carpet, her hands playing with the belt to her robe. She hadn't dressed yet? Excellent.

For once, she had her hair loose too, freshly brushed and hanging past her shoulders. She chewed on her bottom lip. Her continued shyness charmed him.

Booker looked her over, realized she appeared naked beneath the robe, and all kinds of delightful possibilities rolled through him. "Good morning," he murmured, already thinking ahead to how quickly he could get rid of his brother and get Frannie into bed.

Her smile trembled. "Do you remember what you said yesterday, Booker?" Her hands continued to fidget with her belt.

He walked closer. "I said a lot of things."

"You said you wanted me naked."

Heat raced up his spine. "Yeah, I—"

She jerked the belt loose and dropped her robe. It pooled around her slim ankles leaving her gloriously, beautifully nude.

Booker froze, his eyes going wide, his cock leaping to attention. Lord, she devastated his senses. He couldn't blink, couldn't move.

And then from behind him, Axel said, "I don't suppose I should be witnessing this?"

Frannie's screech was shrill enough to shatter glass. The damn robe was on the floor and she dropped down to grab it, twisting at the same time so that her rump faced them instead of her front. And good Lord, the view . . .

Cary coughed. Axel choked.

Belatedly, Booker reeled on his brother. He blasted him with a look and gave him a hard shove that sent him stumbling back into Cary, toppling them both into the kitchen. Neither Axel nor Cary seemed to mind the attack. They were both too busy laughing.

Booker slugged his brother hard in the arm.

"Ow."

"Damn it, Axel, I told you I didn't want you looking at her."

In his defense, Axel said, "I didn't know I'd get to see her in the buff, now did I?" and he rubbed at his shoulder where Booker had hit him. "It's a reflex. Naked woman equals staring. Any man still breathing would look at that, and you damn well know it."

"I would," Cary said, and Booker slugged him, too. But Cary just continued to snicker and grin.

Booker's front door slammed shut.

Damn it! He rounded on his brother again. "Now see what you two have done?"

"Us? We're innocent bystanders. In fact, I think I may have wounded myself when she dropped that robe. My eyeballs hit the floor."

Cary nodded. "Coffee came straight out my nose. Hurt like hell."

Booker pointed a finger at them both. *"Leave."* Then he went into his bedroom and sat on the bed nearest to the wall. He could hear funny noises in Frances's room. Probably her thumping her fists on the bed.

"Frannie?"

The noise stopped, then in an agonized whisper, "I'm going to kill your brother, Booker."

"Not if I kill him first." He smiled. At least she was still talking to him. "Mind if I come over?"

"Yes!"

He rose from the bed, turned—and ran into Axel. After they'd both regained their balance, Booker scowled. "I told you to leave."

"I thought I'd apologize."

Frannie yelled, "Go to hell, Axel!"

Axel grinned. "She's got a temper, doesn't she?"

Booker pushed past him. "Go home, okay?"

He went through his apartment and next door to Frannie's. Her door wasn't locked, so he walked on in, but made a point of locking it behind him.

He found Frances on her bed, facedown, a pillow over her head. She'd pulled the robe back on, but when she'd flung herself on the bed, it had fluttered up to her knees. Her smooth calves and bare feet drew him.

God, he had it bad. "Frances?"

She went utterly still, then gripped the pillow over her head more firmly.

"Are you trying to smother yourself, honey?"

"Maybe," came her muffled reply.

Booker sat on the bed beside her. "I'm sorry you got embarrassed." He was so damn horny, he could barely speak. He wanted to soothe her, to make her feel better, but more than that he wanted to dispense with the robe, turn her to her back and look at her some more. That flash peek at her naked body had only whet an already ravenous appetite.

"Embarrassed?" she repeated with incredulity. "I'm *mortified*. I'll never be able to face your brother again."

Through the wall, Axel said, "That's okay. The rear view was pretty spectacular, too."

Frannie lifted the pillow and stared at the wall with the meanest look Booker had ever seen. Before she could say anything rash, he touched her shoulder. "Ignore Axel. He's an idiot."

"I am," Axel agreed. And then, more sincerely, "I'm sorry I embarrassed you, hon. Booker will beat the hell out of me later, I'm sure, because I bumbled into his fantasy. And I've no doubt you *are* his fantasy. You only have to look at his face when he talks about you."

Frannie twisted about, her narrowed gaze colliding with Booker's heated expression. "Really?"

"Cross my heart."

Axel sighed. "There. All's well that ends well?"

Booker growled. "Will you *go away*, Axel?"

Cary said, "I'll drag him off, Booker. You two just go about your business."

Frannie's expression said, Yeah, right. They both knew Cary and Axel probably had their ears pressed to the wall with no intention of budging.

She was still red-faced, Booker noted, but at least she appeared less murderous. Tired of waiting, Booker scooped her up into his arms and carried her into her living room, away from prying ears. He settled onto the sofa with Frances on his lap. She hadn't turned any lights on yet, so the Christmas tree provided the only real glow in the room. The lights blinked behind her, forming a soft halo against her fair hair.

"I love you, Frances."

She curled into him, hiding her face in his neck. "Even though I just made a gigantic fool of myself?"

"You didn't. You pleased the hell out of me." He smoothed her waist, enjoying the feel of her beneath the terrycloth, the dips and hollows and swells of her body—soon to be his for the taking. Maybe even his forever.

"Axel's right, you know. You are my fantasy, and knowing what you likely intended when you came over to my place has me fully loaded and ready to go." He nibbled on her ear, kissed her temple.

"Yeah?" She wiggled against his erection, letting him know she understood his meaning.

"Damn right. Now if I could just get you to let loose of this robe . . ."

Wearing a beautiful smile, she did, and Booker spread it open so he could look at her to his heart's content. Curled on his lap, every part of her was within reach. Her breasts, her soft belly, her smooth thighs. Those dark blond curls over her mound.

Booker drew a shuddering breath. Physically, he didn't know where to start, where to touch or taste her first.

Emotionally, he knew exactly what he wanted. Gaze glued to her breasts, voice gruff with tenderness, he said, "As long as you're being agreeable, do you suppose you could tell me that you love me, too?"

"I do." He glanced up to find her face rosy with pleasure, anticipation and . . . love. "I have for such a long time."

He hadn't realized he was so tense until her quick agreement sank in. He let out a long breath. "Do you suppose you could agree to marry me?"

"Yes."

She squeaked from his sudden tight embrace, but Booker couldn't seem to loosen his hold. She pressed her palms against him until she could turn on his lap, facing him. She shrugged off the robe, opened his shirt and pressed herself to him chest to chest—heart-to-heart.

Booker's hands roamed freely down her back to her bottom, along the sides of her thighs. Again, he scooped her up, keeping her tight to his chest until he laid her gently on the floor beneath the tree.

As he shrugged off his clothes, his hands already shaking with anticipation, he smiled. "Christmas dinner is going to be interesting." He pulled a condom from his wallet and tossed it to the floor beside her.

"If your brother says one word to me, if he even looks at me funny, I'll clout him."

Booker came down over her. She hadn't refused dinner, and that was all he cared about. He wanted his family to meet her. They'd love her as much as he did. "As I said, interesting."

For several minutes, he simply enjoyed kissing her, touching her. There was no music in the background this time, but Frannie's soft moans and small whimpers were better than any holiday tune.

When he slipped his fingers between her thighs, she arched up. Wet, hot. He stroked two fingers deep, working them in and out of her at a leisurely pace, feeling the grasp and release of her body. Her eyelids sank down, her lips parted.

"Come for me, Frannie." He brought his thumb into play, using her own wetness to glide over her clitoris, softly, easily, repeatedly.

"Booker."

"That's it." He kissed her mouth hard, swallowing her cries, drowning in satisfaction. When she quieted, he rolled the condom on in record time, held her knees high and wide, and pushed into her.

They both groaned.

To Booker's delight, he felt Frances begin tightening all over again. Her short nails stung his shoulders, her runner's thighs held him tight to her. He pumped into her fast, deep—and as she arched high, her mouth open on a raw cry, he came.

Though it was frosty and cold outside, they were both now warm and sweaty. Frances's heart continued to gallop under his cheek. He remained deep inside her, and he never wanted to move.

She was quiet so long, he finally forced himself up to his elbows. Looking at her, at her sated, sleepy contentment, filled his heart to overflowing. "What are you thinking about?"

Lazily she smiled, her eyes opening the tiniest bit. "I got what I wanted for Christmas."

"Me, too."

"But Christmas morning isn't for several more days. I'd like to know just how you plan to top this, Booker Dean. Because I can tell you, it isn't going to be easy."

The grin tugged at his mouth, then won. He laughed out loud. "Oh, I dunno. I think I can come up with something."

"Yeah?"

"Yeah." He lowered himself to kiss her throat,

her flushed breasts, each and every rib. Little by little, he scooted down her body. When he reached his destination, he whispered, "Now this is a gift I won't mind getting every morning for the rest of my life."

With a small moan, Frannie agreed.

SOME LIKE IT HOT

Chapter One

Harsh sunlight found its way through the mini-blinds on the window in exam room four. Though it was well after six, there were no clouds and no breeze to offer relief from the ninety-degree day. Saturday and Sunday promised to be just as stifling. Cary Rupert peeled off his requisite white coat, loosened his tie, and opened the top button of his dress shirt with a sigh.

Maybe the heat could account for his adult patients being so cranky, as well as the incessant whining of his younger patients. Appointments had run two hours over; nothing serious—a summer cold, sunburn, poison ivy rash. Cary was more than ready to head home. He wanted an easy chair, a cold drink, and a smiling, willing woman.

Hell yeah, he'd take all three. Didn't matter

where he got the first two, but the third was a specific craving for one elusive woman. Maybe today he'd finally get lucky.

Leaving his office assistant and two nurses to lock up, Cary stepped outside, a man on a mission. Immediately, he was struck with a wave of hot, humid air. He reached into his breast pocket and fished out his reflective sunglasses for the short walk across the lot to the complex next door, where his best friend, Axel Dean, had an office and where the woman of his dreams worked.

Last year he and Axel had leased space side by side in the new medical complex. As a general practitioner, Cary saw patients of all ages, with just about every ailment under the sun. Axel had specialized as an OB-GYN, so he had only female clientele with the occasional husband or boyfriend stranded in the waiting room. A few spaces down were an ENT and a plastic surgeon. Other various businesses unrelated to medicine filled the complex, and not too many yards away, a Hooters restaurant kept the parking lot packed.

There were no men waiting in Axel's outer office on this late Friday. Cary had no sooner removed his glasses and taken a breath of the air-conditioned lobby air before Axel stuck his head out. "I'll be out of here in ten minutes. You wanna do dinner?"

In doctor mode, Axel was a different person. Serious. Concerned. Attentive to his patients' every word.

Away from the job, he became a complete

hedonist, hysterically funny, and the world's biggest ladies' man. Cary liked him a lot. "Sure thing." Cary cleared his throat and tried to sound casual. "I'll just gab at Nora till you're ready."

Axel rolled his eyes as if he'd expected no less. "She's filing papers in the back," he said, then pointed a finger. "Don't distract her too much. She needs to finish up before she heads home." He ducked back into the hallway and disappeared into an exam room.

Cary's heart beat a little faster in anticipation. From the day he met Nora Chilton eleven months ago, she'd always had that effect on him. She stood five feet, six inches tall, had light brown hair, and kept her soft brown eyes shielded behind librarian-type glasses. Physically, there was nothing to drive a man into a frenzy of lust. But . . . sometimes these things didn't make sense, they just were.

He'd been frenzied from the word jump, and it just kept getting worse, not better. When she smiled, his abdomen clenched as if accepting a punch. Once she'd assisted a pregnant woman to her car, and her gentleness had his pulse tripping. Seeing her in quiet conversation with an expectant father made him tense in what felt too damn much like jealousy. And watching her work, her head bent in just that way, her brows puckered in concentration, caused a slow burn. He loved the way she moved, the gracefulness of her hands, her studious expression behind her glasses.

Five times now he'd asked her out. Five times, she'd declined.

He wanted her, damn it.

She wanted to remain friendly associates.

Sooner or later, Cary knew he'd wear her down, but until then, his life had been filled with frustration of the sexual *and* emotional kind. Lately, he'd turned down so many other women that Axel was starting to give him funny looks. But he didn't want anyone else. He wanted Nora.

Hands deep in his pants pockets, Cary approached the room where his quarry worked. Nora wasn't alone. Before he'd reached the open doorway, Cary heard her chatting with another female. He stuck his head inside and noticed an older woman running a fax machine.

"Hello."

Both women looked up. The older woman smiled. Nora flushed. "Dr. Rupert."

"Cary," he told her, a little peeved that Nora continued to insist on such formality when they were in the office. For crying out loud, there were no patients around, no one to be offended by the fact that they knew each other. Even as he scowled at her, he absorbed her every word. He loved her voice. It was deep and sexy, and she had this crooked way of smiling when she spoke . . .

Nora turned to her coworker to make hasty introductions. "Liza Welch, this is Dr. Rupert. He has an office next door." And with a mere glance at Cary, "Liza started with us a week ago."

Liza reached out. "Nice to meet you, Cary."

He smiled. At least *she* got it right. "Same here, Liza."

She started to say more, but Nora adjusted her glasses and stepped forward. "Can I help you with something?"

Cary stared into those big brown eyes and was lost. He'd meant to just chitchat. He'd meant to just visit her. Instead, he murmured low, "Have dinner with me."

Nora blinked at his husky tone, blushed—and shook her head. "No, I can't. I have work to do."

"Axel's a slave driver." He took two steps into the small room, his gaze glued to hers. "You have to eat. I want the company. *Your* company." And then softer, coaxing, "Have dinner with me."

Her lips parted. Her breath stuttered. And a file slipped right out of her hands, scattering papers everywhere.

Cary backed up a step.

"Oh damn!" Frantic, Nora dropped to her knees to gather the papers. Cary stared at the top of her head. Her hair was cut in short wispy curls that looked adorable and exposed her nape—a nape he wanted to touch and kiss. She was dressed in a shapeless white nurse's uniform, and somehow even that looked sexy, despite the rubber-soled shoes.

Jesus, he had it bad.

He knelt down to help.

At his nearness, Nora rushed into a speech, turning him down once again. "Really, Dr. Rupert." She snatched a paper right out of his hand. "I'm so busy and I don't have time to talk right now. It's going to take me forever to sort this again."

Insulted, Cary pushed back to his feet. She

stood, too, the mangled papers clutched to her chest. She looked pugnacious and put out and so damn cute, it irritated him.

"I'm sorry I interrupted." In a huff, he stalked out.

To hell with it. He wouldn't ask her again. Of course, he'd told himself that before, but whenever he saw her, the invitation just came out of his mouth, without his permission, without coherent intent from him. She muddled him and made him hot and destroyed his ego with her persistent cold shoulder.

When he didn't hit on her, she was as pleasant as could be. But let him even hint that he wanted more than friendship, and she shot him down real fast.

Cary had his head lowered, chewing over his turbulent thoughts, when he literally ran into Axel.

"Whoa." Axel, tall and strong and equally stubborn, stumbled back into a wall. "Where the hell are you going?"

Cary slashed a hand through the air. "Out."

"Out?"

Shit. He didn't want Axel in his private business, privy to his turmoil. They shared a lot, but not that, not rejection. Axel never got rejected, which guaranteed he'd find Cary's situation entertaining and fodder for endless prodding.

Cary thought fast and came up with a lame but plausible excuse. "I'm going to start my car so it can cool off. It must be like an oven inside with this damned heat wave."

"Great idea." Axel thwacked him on the

shoulder, hard enough to be retaliation for the way Cary had run into him moments earlier. "Grab my keys out of my office and start mine, too, will you? I'll be ready in just a couple of minutes, I swear."

"Why not?" Cary turned around and retraced his steps to reach Axel's office. He was glaring toward the room where Nora and the other woman worked when, as he got closer, he heard their voices, and this time the conversation was much more . . . titillating.

"Why in the world would you turn a stud-muffin like that down?" Liza demanded.

Stud muffin? Cary flattened himself against the wall beside the door.

"I have to work."

"Yeah, right," Liza said. "And I'm a nun. You'll have to tell that tale to someone younger or dumber than me, because honey, I've been around the block."

Cary could hear the smile in Nora's tone when she replied. "You're only fifty, not a wizened hundred."

"Fifty is a lot of years to watch human nature. That young buck scares you."

"No."

"Yes," Liza insisted. "And I'm nosy enough to want to know why."

He scared Nora? Ears cocked like a bloodhound, Cary waited to hear more.

Nora's sigh of exasperation was extreme. Papers rustled, the fax machine dialed. "I'm widowed."

Widowed! But she was in her midtwenties—too young to be married, much less widowed.

Liza snorted. "I know, but you're very much alive."

How come Liza knew, but no one had ever told him?

"And," Liza continued, "given the way Cary was looking at you, it's for sure you'd have a great time if you just gave him a chance."

"A good time, maybe. But I want what I had. A husband, not a lover. The promise of home and hearth, not just sex." Nora sighed. "And I want kids."

Chuckling, Liza said, "Now, I may have just met him, but that young man looked more than potent enough to give you a dozen babies if you want them."

Cary's eyes nearly crossed. Babies? With Nora? He thought of her pregnant, maybe breast-feeding, holding an infant that looked like him or her or both.

"Capable, sure, but willing?"

Hell yeah.

"Maybe you should ask him," Liza suggested.

Yeah, ask me. Ask me.

"No need. If you'd ever heard the way Cary goes on about children, you'd know how he feels on that subject. After a long day of treating them, he makes it clear how glad he is *not* to have any of his own."

Liza was undaunted by that fact. "So until you meet this paragon of husband material, why not have some fun with the willing doctor?"

Cary held his breath. The silence stretched out so long, he almost suffocated himself.

Then, in a small voice, Nora said, "What if I fall in love with him? No, Liza, I'm serious. I'm not the type to have an affair. I was a virgin when I married, and I haven't been with anyone since."

"You're kidding, right?" Liza's tone sounded disbelieving. "When did your husband die?"

"Two years ago. We were married only six months. Not long enough. I miss him still."

Heart in his throat, Cary moved to stand in the open doorway. Liza had just reached for Nora and embraced her. "Shame on me for bringing it all back up. I'm sorry."

Cary stared at Nora and said, "I'm not."

The file fell out of her hands again.

Liza laughed and shook a finger at Cary. "You've had your ear to the wall, haven't you?"

"More or less." He wouldn't lie about it. He may have been a reprobate—almost as bad as Axel—but he would never lie to Nora.

"Well, you two go on and talk it out." Liza winked at Cary. "I'll get this file put away."

Before she could react to that suggestion, Cary wrapped his fingers around Nora's upper arm. She was stiff, silent. "Good idea."

"No." Belatedly, Nora found her voice, although it was little more than a whisper. She pulled back, but Cary already had her through the doorway. He'd been headed to Axel's office, so he continued on his way there, urging Nora inside and shutting the thick door behind them.

He turned to face her, considered everything he wanted to say. But she was just standing there, her arms folded over her middle, her soft mouth trembling, her cheeks hot. And he jumped the gun.

He kissed her.

Nora didn't have time to react. She'd done her best to block out his warm masculine scent, to ignore how fine he looked with his shirt-sleeves rolled up and his tie loose. His visual appeal got to her every time, but she'd been resisting it for almost a year now. His brown hair, shades darker than her own, was immaculately trimmed but always disheveled in a very boyish way. His green eyes were teasing and they made her feel both lighthearted and needy.

She'd been prepared to hear his coaxing voice, to withstand the intensity of his warm appraisal.

But she hadn't even considered a kiss. At least not now, not in the office. God knew she'd spent too many nights imagining what it'd be like, but she'd assumed it'd never happen.

It had happened now. And the second his warm, firm mouth touched hers, coherent thought evaporated. Her mind felt sluggish, her skin far too sensitive, while her heart pounded fast and hard, making her struggle for breath. Mercy!

It wasn't an invasive kiss. It was gentle and sweet, soft and lingering. Her toes curled.

Cary hovered so close she didn't dare open

her eyes or she'd be caught. They shared breath. His scent wrapped around her. His body heat added to the heat of the day and her own turbulence.

"Nora," he whispered, and his big hand curled around her nape, caressing, keeping her close. His palm was hot, too. Everything about the man sizzled. "Kiss me back."

She drew a stuttering breath. "I . . ." *Don't know how.* No, she couldn't say something that stupid. But it had been so many years, the memories of kissing had long since faded. The need remained, but the mechanics were vague. "I'm sorry."

His forehead touched hers, displacing her glasses. "I'm not giving up."

She almost laughed. For the length of time she'd known Cary, he'd been gently persistent, crawling under her skin and into her dreams, and not a day went by that she didn't think of him. During the week, he found one reason or another to come to the office and talk with her. At every social event, he sought her out. "I know."

"I do so like kids."

That sudden disclosure startled her. "What?"

He raised his head, gave her a long look, then straightened her glasses with a small smile. "When I bitch about it, that's just exhaustion talking. If I didn't love kids, I wouldn't work so hard to keep them healthy."

Heat rushed into her face. "You said plain as day you didn't want any."

He rolled one shoulder. "Men say that crap all the time. It's nothing, just hot air meant to bloat our images as bachelors." Then, more firmly, "I want kids. *Someday.*" And softly, "With the right woman."

Why did he have to look at her like that while saying such a thing? Nora tried to back up, but her shoulder blades were already touching the door. "Your *someday* is probably ten years away."

Eyes narrowed in consideration, Cary looked her over. "Will you go to dinner with me tonight?"

She almost swallowed her tongue at the quick change in subject. "What does that have to do with you and kids?"

There was that small smile again, teasing her senses, melting her heart. "I can't start figuring out when someday will be until I start making headway with you."

Nora dropped back against the door; she needed it for support. "You just want to have sex."

"With you? Damn right." He braced his hands on the door at either side of her head. "Bad."

Somehow, her heart was up in her throat, choking off her breath. She stared up at him, and got snared.

Cary brushed a kiss to her chin. "Knowing you've been celibate two years just honed the knife." He kissed her cheekbone beneath the armature of her glasses.

"Knife?" she squeaked.

"The one that cuts me every time I think of lying down with you." His breath warmed her neck, then his mouth was there, damp, gently sucking.

"Oh." She literally panted. Without really considering it, she put her hands up against his chest—and froze at the delightful feel of solid muscles beneath fine linen. She could feel his heartbeat, too—hard, slow, and steady.

"I want you bad enough that it hurts, Nora. Tell me yes."

He kissed his way up to her ear, leaving a damp, molten path behind on her neck. His tongue touched her lobe, prodded just inside, and her knees almost gave out. *"Yes."*

Grasping her shoulders, Cary lurched back to see her face. "Really?"

Uh-oh. Nora blinked fast, bringing herself back to reality. What had she said? "Ummm . . ."

His hold tightened. "No, never mind. I heard it." His grin stretched from ear to ear. "Tonight?"

Tonight. Tonight. "No, I, uh . . . I'm beat, Cary. I just want to go home and take a swim and then relax." *I want to go home and guard my heart.*

His brows pulled down. "Then tomorrow?"

She started to shake her head—and Axel shoved the door open. She stumbled into Cary; his arms went around her, bringing her even closer, breasts to chest, belly to groin. He groaned, the sound both excited and pained.

"What the hell?" Like a bull, Axel pressed in, forcing them out of his way. His eyes darted from Nora to Cary and back again. One brow arched high when he saw their embrace. "Playing doctor in my office, huh? Can't you rendezvous in your own? It's right next door."

Flustered, almost speechless, Nora shoved away from Cary. "We were just . . . we were . . . talking."

"Yeah, that's what it looked like." Axel's gaze moved over her red face. "Talking."

"Shut up, Axel." Cary caught her arm. "I'll call you tonight."

Because Nora didn't know what else to do, she fashioned a smile and nodded agreement. She'd rather deal with Cary on the phone than in person any day. Over the phone, she'd only hear his mouth, not feel it or taste it. "Fine." She turned to Axel, knew her face was crimson, and brazened it out. "If you're ready to lock up, I'll just go get my purse."

She literally fled the office, aware of both men watching her, aware of her own awkwardness. It had been far, far too long since she'd dealt with an interested male. Never had she dealt with a man like Cary Rupert.

Liza stepped out into the hall, intercepting her escape. "Everything settled?"

Not about to linger for any reason, Nora grabbed her and dragged her in her wake. In the short week that Liza had worked with her, they'd become close. Liza was relaxed and easy to be with, if a little too pushy at times, but she was also very caring and incredible with the patients. "Come on. Time to head home." Nora wanted to be long gone before Axel and Cary made it outside.

Liza laughed. "Running like the hounds of hell were on your heels. Or is it just one sexy hound you're worried about?"

"I'm not worried," she lied. She was terrified.

"You're worried you'll fall in love with him. You told me so."

Nora shook her head. She knew the awful truth: she'd been in love with Cary Rupert for months. Now that he knew why she fought it, what would he do?

She bit her lip. "I'm not going to talk about this anymore. I'm going home for a dip in the pool. The water isn't cold anymore, but at least it's relaxing."

"A cold shower would be better," Liza told her with a grin.

"Maybe," she agreed, accepting Liza's triumphant laugh. But she knew a cold shower wouldn't do the trick, either. She wanted Cary, now more than ever. And the wanting wouldn't go away anytime soon, because Cary wouldn't go away.

He wanted only sex. She wanted it all.

And Nora Chilton was not a woman who settled for half measures. She just had to keep reminding herself of that, especially now that Cary had turned up the heat.

Chapter Two

"So you and Nora have something going on, huh? And you weren't going to tell me?"

Cary turned away from Axel and started out of the office. Damn it, that hadn't gone quite as he'd hoped.

Axel followed along. Like a dog with a meaty bone, he kept chewing. "Never mind that we're friends. Best friends, in case you've forgotten. And Nora works for me. She's my responsibility—"

Cary whipped around. "No way."

Smiling now that he had Cary's attention, Axel said, "Way."

"Don't even think it, Axel. I mean it."

Axel laughed. "What's this? You struck out, but you're afraid I'll hit a home run?" He threw his arm around Cary and dragged him out the door. "Relax, man. I draw the line at fooling around with females in my employ. You know that."

Cary did know it, but lust had helped him to forget. "Yeah, I know." And he added, "Sorry."

"Appreciate the vote of confidence, by the way." They paused beside Axel's new BMW. Axel put on his sunglasses and stared up at the sky. "The glasses didn't throw you off?"

With his mind still buzzing from Nora's nearness, the feel of her, her taste, Cary was slow to achieve coherency. "What?"

"Her glasses. I mean, even if you overlook the short hair—"

"It's sort of a Halle Berry thing, don't you think?"

"—and those shapeless uniforms—"

"Which *you* insist she wear."

"—she still looks . . . I dunno. Studious."

Cary tried that word on for size. "Yeah, studious fits her. She's smart."

"Of course she is. I wouldn't hire a dumb woman."

"No, I mean beyond being a nurse. We've talked about everything from politics to family values, and she always makes sense. Unlike some people I know." He gave Axel a sharp look, so he'd understand whom he meant.

Axel ignored the insult. "She's nothing at all like a bombshell, which since you still appear dumbfounded, I'll point out is the type of woman you usually gravitate to."

Actually, that was the type of woman Axel preferred. Cary just went along for the ride. He grinned at his own sexual pun. Too many times, they'd picked up women together. Not strangers, but friends, acquaintances, sisters . . . Casual sex had lost its appeal a long time ago. Now he wanted more. He wanted Nora. "She's sexy."

Dubious in the extreme, Axel said, "You think?"

"You don't?"

Axel eyed him. "I'm not stupid enough to disagree with a besotted man. If you say it's so, then it must be."

Cary bristled—until he realized that he sure as hell didn't want Axel to start lusting after her, too. Talk about awkward. He slapped his friend on the arm. "Wise man."

"Yeah, so wise that I'm standing here on blacktop, in sweltering heat, trying to figure out how to tell you that you're an idiot."

Sweat trickled down Cary's temple. He swiped his forearm over his brow. "So just spit it out."

"She wants you, you want her. Why are you planning on having dinner with me?"

"She turned me down."

"So?" With typical Axel mentality, he said, "Seduce her."

"You are such a Neanderthal."

"Cajole her. Reason with her. Go to her house and spill your guts." Axel unlocked his car and pulled the driver's door open. Heat rolled out in a suffocating wave. "Get laid—and then maybe you can be worthwhile company again."

Now there was a thought. She'd said she wanted a swim . . . Cary's brain stalled at the image of Nora in a swimsuit with lots of skin showing. Almost to himself, Cary said, "I know where she lives." Her neighborhood wasn't that far from his.

"So what are you waiting for?" Axel gave him a shove. "Go before you start sweating like a pig and gross her out. But if this screws up my office dynamics, I'll kick your ass."

Cary saluted him and headed on his way. He heard Axel muttering about friends who didn't even say good-bye anymore, but he paid little attention to Axel as his thoughts leaped forward. Would Nora let him in? Would she give him a chance to spill his guts?

The idea of seducing her appealed to him in a big way. Cary got behind the wheel of his SUV and considered his options. By rote, he started the engine and turned the air on full blast before putting the vehicle in drive.

Nora had been pretty pliable in the office, all because of one small kiss. How would she react to him touching her breasts, her belly? What would she do when he sank his fingers into her, making her wetter, making him hotter? He drew a shaky breath. She said she'd been two years without sex—she had to be primed, so it'd be easy . . .

But no, that wasn't fair to do to her. His hands clenched on the steering wheel. Damn it, he didn't just want her carried away for the moment. He wanted her to want him, today and tomorrow and next month. Like Nora, he wanted more than a fling.

He was almost to her home before the air-conditioning finally cooled down the interior.

Not that he'd noticed much. The heat inside him put the sultry day to shame.

Parking at the curb, he got out and surveyed her house. Small, neat, a Cape Cod with roses growing everywhere. She had a sprinkler going in the front yard, a summer wreath of flowers on the door. It looked homey. It looked like Nora, like what he wanted with her.

A knock on the front door brought no results. Stymied, Cary thought about it a moment, then remembered her pool. Disregarding formality, he walked around back, his hands in his pockets, his reflective sunglasses shielding his eyes from the low-hanging sun. And there was Nora.

Christ Almighty, she looked good.

Cary drew to a halt and just stared. Like crystals, setting sunlight danced on the water around her. She rested on her back atop a float, her glasses gone, her short hair wet and slicked back—her belly showing.

She was relaxed, limp, drifting in the small, rectangular in-ground pool. One hand rested above her head, the other trailed in the water. Her peach-colored suit was by no means a bikini, but the modest two-piece suited her. It was wet, clinging to her breasts so that the plump shape of her nipples showed. Cary stiffened his thighs, locked his knees. He wanted her in his mouth. He wanted to feast on those nipples and hear her cry out, feel her moving against him.

With an effort, he got a grip on himself and continued his perusal.

The swimsuit's bottom was wide, but still rode beneath her belly button and was cut high on her thighs. He could see the rise of her mound, the tender inside of her thighs.

She wore sunscreen, because she was creamy pale all over, her fair complexion emphasizing her femaleness.

Knowing he couldn't continue to stand there like a voyeur, Cary forced himself forward, moving silently on the lush lawn until he stood at the very edge of the concrete pool.

"Nora."

She jerked so hard she fell off her raft, legs and arms pedaling, sending a splash of water onto Cary's shoes. When her head resurfaced, she sputtered, then squinted toward him, one hand shielding her eyes while she tried to see him without her glasses. "Cary?"

"Yeah." He sounded hoarse, but damn, he was getting hard already just looking at her. Water droplets beaded on her shoulders—and her nipples were no longer soft.

As if she'd only just realized that herself, she crossed her arms over her chest. "My . . . my glasses are up there somewhere."

Cary located them on a lawn chair beneath a towel and knelt down to hand them to her. "Here you go."

She bit her lip, hesitated, and inched forward. Breathless, she said, "Thanks." Maybe hesitant to face him, she slid the glasses on with slow precision. She kept her head bent. "I wasn't expecting you."

"I know."

She swallowed, breathed fast, and finally, with excruciating slowness, raised her face.

Cary pulled off his sunglasses. He wanted her to see his eyes, to know what he felt. "Can I join you?"

Her jaw loosened and her mouth fell open.

"My briefs will look like trunks to your neighbors, if any of them can even see us here."

She looked from one side of her privacy fence to the other. "Neighbors?"

Her confusion charmed him. Gently, he explained, "There are houses, so there must be people living in them."

She nodded.

Making the decision for her, Cary stood and unbuttoned his shirt. Her big doe eyes widened even more, and a pulse thrummed wildly in her throat. Her fascinated gaze tracked his progress, button to button, the widening of material, until he pulled the shirttails from his slacks and shrugged it off his shoulders. The sun on his bare skin felt good after the long day, and he stretched before putting the shirt on the back of the chair.

"Oh."

She liked his chest? He *loved* hers. Going to the lawn chair, Cary sat down and pulled off his shoes and socks. "Is the water cold?"

She shook her head, still watching him with absorbed attention.

"Pity." He stood, unbuckled his belt, drew down his zipper—and dropped his pants. There wasn't a damn thing he could do about his boner, barely constrained by the snug, black cotton boxers.

Nora stared, drew a broken breath, and licked her lips. Did she know what that small lick did to him?

She turned and swam to the other side of the pool, keeping her back to him.

Cary dove in. The initial force of his entry carried him across the pool so that he surfaced right behind her. She gripped the side of the pool, her toes balanced on a ledge.

Cary mimicked her stance, putting his hands alongside hers, his feet bracketing hers on the ledge. His cock pressed into her firm bottom. If they were naked, he could enter her this way, leaving his hands free to play with her breasts while he thrust deep and slow . . . He turned his face into her neck. "Nora."

As if she'd had the same imagery, she moaned.

Opening his mouth, Cary took a slow love bite of the muscle running from her neck to her shoulder. "I want you." He felt her shiver. "More than you can even begin to guess."

"You . . . you don't want to get married," she whispered.

She was so damn sure of that. And if he told her now, at this particular moment, with an erection prodding her backside, that he wanted marriage and forever after and those kids she'd mentioned earlier, she'd think he was just on the make. She'd think he was making promises just to get laid.

He drew back a little, giving them both some breathing room. But not much, because he couldn't bear the distance between them. "We haven't even been on a real date yet, so how do you know what I want? With you, everything is different."

"You're so determined. But . . . why me?"

He shook his head. "Hell, Nora, that's like asking why I like chocolate ice cream better than vanilla, or why I prefer boxers to briefs, or why I bought an SUV instead of a flashy car."

She turned in his arms. Her glasses were now wet with droplets of water, but her eyes were direct. "And?"

"And what?"

"Why did you make those choices?"

They were both mostly naked. For all intents and purposes, they were alone. It wasn't easy for him to concentrate. "Maybe we should move to your patio for this discussion?"

She nodded—then waited. When Cary just stood there, breathing in the scent of her warmed skin, her wet hair, and the light fragrance that was all woman and hers alone, she cleared her throat. "You need to . . . move, so I can get out."

"Oh. Yeah." He stepped to the side of her, hoisted himself out, then reached in for her. Catching her wrists, he pulled her up and against him. She fit him perfectly, her head at just the right height for his shoulder.

As naturally as if they'd been a couple forever, he put his arm around her waist and walked her around the pool to her towel. She didn't dry off with it. Instead, she wrapped it around herself, hiding her body from him.

Okay, he could deal with that. For right now. He gathered up his clothes and shoes, then reached out a hand, and after a long moment of hesitation, she took it.

Cary led her to the middle of her covered patio. Wet and shaded, he felt cooler on the outside, but no less hot on the inside. He set his clothes and shoes down. They stared at each other. With one finger, he touched her mouth. "Chocolate tastes better to me—just as you taste better."

Her lashes lowered and new color stained her cheeks.

He coasted that same finger down her shoulder to the swell of her breasts, visible above the tightly wrapped towel. "Boxers," he murmured while tugging the towel free of its knot, "are more comfortable." He dropped the towel on the concrete patio. Everything about her, from her hesitation to her sweet little body, turned him on.

"You're saying I'm comfortable?"

"Yeah. Being with you feels right."

She wet her lips.

After a leisurely, heated review of her body, Cary met her gaze, his expression as intent as he could make it so that she'd understand. "Flashy cars don't appeal to me anymore." He caught her waist and drew her close again. "They're just for fun, but these days I'm more interested in the long haul."

Her lips parted, but just before Cary could kiss her, she drew back. Frustration rose up—at himself for rushing her again. Damn it, around her it seemed that his dick wanted to call all the shots, never mind what his brain had to say about it. "I'm sorry."

Shaking her head, Nora said, "I have to explain."

"All right."

She kept her gaze on his chest while visibly working up her nerve. In a voice so small, Cary could barely hear her, she confessed, "I was a virgin when I married."

Her husband must have had one hell of a wedding night. Bending his knees, Cary tried to see her face, but she only tucked her chin in a little more.

"My husband was a virgin, too. What we knew, we learned together."

Cary released her, turned his back on her, and took three deep breaths, then a fourth and a fifth. Jealousy raged inside him, though he doubted that was her intent. "I can't miraculously become a virgin, Nora."

Her startled, nervous laugh had him turning back around again with bemused curiosity at her reaction. One hand covered her mouth, but her eyes were still smiling. Cary smiled, too. "Want me to pretend to be?"

Another laugh bubbled out. "No." She swatted at him playfully. "Don't be ridiculous."

"Good." The sound of her laughter filled him up when he hadn't really known he was empty. "I doubt I could have pulled it off anyway."

She swallowed, cleared her throat, and tried to be serious again. Rushing to get it all out, she blurted, "I haven't been with anyone in two years."

"I know." His cock throbbed in renewed interest. Two long years. Damn. Talking about it only made it more real. "I heard you tell Liza that," he reminded her.

"Not even a kiss."

His brain went blank. *Not even . . .*

"Not even . . . holding hands."

"Jesus, Nora, why?" Cary could hardly credit such a thing. "You're beautiful and sexy. I know damn good and well guys have been asking. Hell, *I've* been asking." If she told him she was still in love with her husband, after all this time, he'd howl.

She half turned away from him, giving him her profile. "At first, I didn't want anyone else because I missed my husband too much."

There it was, the one thing he couldn't fight— a dead man. "I can understand that, but it's been *two years.*"

She rubbed her forehead, readjusted her glasses. "I was always really shy with men."

The small voice was back, proving to Cary that this was a difficult topic for her. He moved closer, giving her silent support.

"Dating didn't come easy to me." She flashed him a quick look to see if he understood. "We dated for eighteen months before we married."

Eighteen months of celibate dating? Wow.

"Even after we married, I felt awkward sleeping with my husband." She bit her lip and squeezed her eyes shut. "I don't . . ." She gestured toward him with a hand. "Anything I know about sex I learned with my husband."

Cary was starting to understand. Two virgins fumbling in the dark added up to a lack of confidence in the sack. "And it wasn't all that much that you learned?"

"Exactly." Eyes still closed, she said, "But it wasn't his fault. He loved me and we were both innocent, but I just—"

He stepped behind her, put her hands on her waist. "Did you ever have an orgasm?"

She trembled.

"Nora?"

In a barely there whisper, she said, "No." Then in a rush, "But I loved him, Cary. A lot."

"Shhh. It's all right. I understand." He understood that her husband had been cheated out of a lot of pleasure by dying too young. And Nora had been cheated, too. In a big way.

So what the hell should he do now?

She was a nurse for an OB-GYN. She dealt with pregnant ladies—the result of sex, no two ways about that—every damn day. His brain churned, trying to muddle out the situation. "Do you believe that I care about you, Nora?"

"I don't know."

Well, there was honesty for you. "I do. I wouldn't lie to you." He was caressing her waist without realizing it. Her skin was so silky soft he couldn't wait to feel all of it against him while they made love. "How did your husband die?"

"Massive heart attack. I . . . I woke up one morning and he was . . . he was gone. I didn't hear anything, didn't know he'd had a problem in the night."

Woke up? "He was beside you? In bed?"

She nodded.

Damn. No wonder she hadn't wanted to rush into any other man's bed. Cary turned her, hauled her into his arms, and kissed her. Not a gentle kiss this time, but one of hunger and need and possession. He hurt for her and wished for some way to erase those memories from her mind, even while he sought a way to claim her.

She wasn't really kissing him back, but her hands clutched his shoulders and he could feel her fast breaths. "Give me your tongue."

She parted her lips, shyly did as he ordered—and Cary was lost. He drew her soft pink tongue into his mouth, sucked gently, teased with his own and followed her tongue back into her mouth, licking, tasting. Hot. Damn, she was hot.

The kiss went on and on, sharing, taking, giving. It required all his concentration to keep his hands on her waist and not lift them to her breasts, or drop them to her bottom. It was enough that he could feel her skin, wet from her swim, warm from the summer day.

Slowly, before he pushed too far too fast, he pulled back. She struggled to get her heavy eyelids lifted, then her gaze locked with his and her tongue flicked out, tasting her lips. "I liked that."

She wasn't helping his self-control, saying things like that. He cupped her face. "You'll like everything I do to you, I swear. We'll be incredible together, Nora."

Her mouth twitched into a small, nervous smile. "Great sex, that's what you're offering?"

"*No.*"

She looked confused. "No?"

Cary groaned. What the hell was he saying? "I mean, yeah, but more than that, okay?"

He wanted her to ask him how much more, but she didn't. With her thoughts clear on her expressive face, she considered everything he said, touched one hot little palm to his chest, and whispered, "Okay."

Such a rush of triumph, expectation, and tenderness rolled through him, it was almost like coming, almost as sweet. But not quite. "Now?" *Please let her mean now.*

Her big brown eyes looked up at him from behind her glasses. She gave a tiny nod, smiled tremulously, and said, "Okay." And then to confirm it, "Now."

Chapter Three

Cary wasn't a gallant man or a guy prone to melodrama. Never in his life had he carried a woman to bed. Hell, he was more likely to race her there, laughing with every step. But now, with Nora, he felt like a cross between Tarzan and a groom on his wedding day. He felt like the Initiator of Virgins and it was such a turn-on, he could barely draw breath.

He lifted her up high against his chest, caught her small sound of exclamation, and kissed her. He could kiss her forever, every day, every hour even. "You won't be sorry, I swear. I'll make this so good for you."

"I know."

When he reached the French doors, she pulled them open and Cary swept inside, a romantic figure to the core. "Which way?"

Appearing a tad overwhelmed, Nora said, "Um, down the hall, last door on the right."

It wasn't easy, but he accomplished a sedate walk rather than a run. He even kissed her twice again without getting carried away. He didn't stop and take her against the wall, or on the floor, as was his basic inclination, given the level of his need.

Her bedroom door stood open, her bed unmade and rumpled. "Wet suits," Cary told her, forcing himself to be logical. This was almost like her first time, close enough that he wanted it to be special, so close he was the one trembling like a virgin—with anticipation. Sopping sheets would add nothing to the ambiance for either of them. He stood her on her feet to strip her.

She shied away—but he drew her right back. "I want to see you, Nora. All of you. And I want you to see me."

"You do?"

Trying to curb the drumming of lust, he said, "Of course I do. I've dreamed of seeing you naked."

Heat flared in her cheeks. "But you want me to see you, too?"

See me, touch me, lick me . . . He groaned. "Yeah."

"Oh."

He cleared his throat. "I want you to want me."

"I do."

Thank God. He angled closer, reached behind her, and slowly unhooked her bra top. The cups loosened from her breasts. He untied the string around her neck and the bathing suit top fell between them. Cary pulled it away and dropped it to the carpet. He couldn't breathe. Her breasts were . . . well, they were Nora's breasts, soft and pale, her nipples puckered tight. He bent and drew one into his mouth, sucking gently.

With pleasure as much as embarrassment, Nora gasped. Her hands settled in his hair, tangled there, held him tight. Cary spread his hands wide over her back to keep her close. Her skin was cool in the air-conditioned interior, soft and sleek. He spanned her waist, her hips. Gliding his fingers into her trunks, he pushed them off her rounded bottom, then went to one knee and tugged them the rest of the way down her legs.

Bad move.

He was now eye level with her belly, or more importantly, her soft pubic curls. She was still damp from the swim. Her scent was delicious, making him want so much more, far too soon.

She pressed her thighs tight together and covered herself with her hands.

Hoarse, Cary said, "Step out of your bottoms."

She did, awkwardly, her limbs stiff, her hands still shielding her from his gaze. Seeing her hands there just brought about a ton of sexual fantasies. He should have stood back up at that point, but he couldn't. He cupped her bare, plump bottom, kneaded her for a moment while he argued with himself—and lost.

He leaned forward and kissed her knuckles.

"Cary."

Holding her close, he used his tongue to trace between her fingers, down, back up, flicking just a bit over the middle knuckle of her right hand. He wished she'd part her fingers just a bit, maybe let him . . .

She stumbled back against the mattress.

In a red haze of lust, Cary stood and looked at her. She now had one hand covering her left breast, the other hand over her sex, and he was so hard he could have been lethal. Holding her gaze, he shoved his clinging wet boxers down and off, then kicked them away. He straightened, letting her look her fill.

She nearly went cross-eyed as she stared fixedly at his face.

"Look at me, Nora."

After a few breaths to shore her up, her gaze darted to his erection for a two-second peek. But apparently that didn't suffice, because her attention shot downward again, where it lingered and warmed. Her lips parted.

Hoarse, Cary murmured, "Let me feel you." He removed her glasses and set them on the nightstand, then carried her trembling hands to his shoulders. This time when he pulled her into his arms, there were no barriers. Flesh to flesh, heartbeat to heartbeat. Her nipples rubbed his ribs, her thighs shifted against his. His swollen cock nudged against her silky belly.

He felt cocooned in her softness, her musky female scent, her timidity and sex appeal. He closed his eyes and pressed his face into her throat, overcome with emotions he'd never dealt with before. He wanted to ravish her. He wanted to absorb her into himself.

He had to keep his head to ensure she enjoyed this. He wanted her to see how wonderful their lovemaking would be. He wanted her to crave more, of him and the pleasure he'd give her.

Taking her mouth with premeditated tenderness, Cary lowered them both to the bed. For long minutes, he just kissed her, sometimes rolling on top of her so she could become accustomed to his weight, sometimes turning so she was atop him, letting her move as she pleased. He kissed her gently, not so gently, deep and slow, wild and wet. But he kept his hands on safe ground—her shoulders, her waist. He held her face, smoothed her hair, teased her nape. And when she was quivering, filling his head with small gasps and making him nuts with the way she writhed against him, he laid her on her back and cupped her breasts.

She arched, firming his hold, giving him more. She was firm, round, and so damn soft. Cary kissed his way down her throat, her chest, until his mouth again closed over one taut nipple.

"Oh God."

Her fingers held his skull, drawing him closer, encouraging him. With leisurely intent, he suckled one nipple while plying the other with his thumb. He shook worse than she did. Restraint, he discovered, was not an easy thing. In fact, it was pure hell. Especially now, because he'd never suffered this level of burning lust before. And here he'd thought he knew all about it. Damn, but it was different with Nora. Hotter and sweeter, so intense. His whole body strained to be closer, to be inside her.

He knew he wouldn't be able to wait much longer, and he needed to know if she was ready. He pressed his hand between their bodies, low on her belly, his fingers splayed. She didn't freeze up on him. In fact, she squirmed, trying to get his fingers where she wanted them. Cary lifted up and looked at her face. Eyes closed, head tilted back, she appeared wanton and ready. Utterly beautiful.

"You'll like this," he told her. With the heel of his palm pressed to the top of her mound, he petted her with his fingertips, slow, easy, gentle. Just stroking.

She moaned and lifted her hips.

With his middle finger, he parted her—and felt her distended clitoris, ripe and ready, so sensitive. She was creamy wet, swollen, very near the edge. Heat raged through him. He locked his jaw, tensed his shoulders against the driving need, and stroked with just one fingertip, teasing, easing her deeper into the moment.

"Cary," she whispered on a thin breath of sound, then her back arched hard and she gave a long, raw moan.

Like a wire pulled too tight, Cary snapped. Two fingers sank deep into her, pulled out, and thrust again, preparing her, widening her. She was so tight, her inner muscles clasping at his fingers, that he knew he'd die when he got inside her.

Before he even knew what he was doing, he

was over her, catching her knees, pulling her legs apart. He couldn't breathe, couldn't think—hell, he couldn't even see straight. But he felt her small frantic hands, dragging him down so she could kiss and lick his mouth, her silken thighs wrapping tight around him.

Blindly, he positioned himself and thrust hard.

She bowed beneath him, crying out but clinging to him, adding to the urgency. Cary pressed, retreated, pressed until he was buried deep, as deep as he could go. He rode her hard, no rubber, no soft sex words, just savage, pounding need. Less than a shameful minute later he was coming, so hard and long that he shouted at his release, his head thrown back like a wild man, his hands knotted tight into the sheets beneath her, every muscle straining.

When the spasms finally left him long moments later, he fell heavily onto her, incoherent, damn near unconscious. He thought he might have been breathing, but he wasn't sure. Little sparks of pleasure continued to snap inside him, making him twitchy.

An indeterminable amount of time passed before he became aware of Nora's nose touching his shoulder, her deep inhalations, the restless way she moved beneath him.

Oh shit!

He'd just mauled her.

Ravaged her.

She hadn't come at all, at least not that he'd noticed amid all his shouting and groaning and

straining. He had, though. Hell, he'd blown like
Mt. Vesuvius after an extended dry spell.

And he hadn't worn a rubber. *Oh shit, oh shit.*

Cary swallowed. *Sit up,* he told himself, but he
didn't move. He wasn't sure he could move yet.

And then Nora whispered, "You smell so
good," and she nuzzled her nose against his
sweaty shoulder again.

With Herculean effort, Cary rolled to the side
of her. Or maybe it was more that he flopped
like a half-dead fish. Nora didn't follow. She
didn't move at all. She just stared at the ceiling—and the damn silence suffocated him.

Cary waited for his heart to slow just a bit
more, then he choked down his embarrassment
and said, "Yeah, uh, that didn't go quite like I
planned."

Silence.

"That's, uh, never happened to me before."
So lame.

Her big eyes closed, shutting him out. "Sorry."

He did a double take. His brow cocked.
"What's that?"

"I'm sorry. I told you I wasn't good at . . ."
Her hand moved, fluttered above the bed, then
resettled on the mattress. "This stuff."

Oh, hell no. New energy flowed into Cary,
enough that he could prop himself up on one
elbow. Progress, he thought, as the tingling in
his limbs faded. At least his mind was function-
ing again. He surveyed Nora, and liked what he
saw. No, he *loved* what he saw.

Her short hair was still slightly damp, in cute

little curls around her face. Her cheeks were rosy. Little tremors coursed through her—the effects of going unfulfilled, no doubt. Her nipples were darkly flushed, still taut. Hmmm. "You're kidding, right?"

Her jaw worked before the words came out. "I can't . . . can't seem to . . ."

Idly, as if he didn't have a care in the world, Cary reached for her breast and toyed with her nipple. Her hands clenched and she moaned. "Nora, listen to me."

"I can't." Her whole body was rigid, stiff. "Not while you're doing that."

Smiling, Cary put his hand on her belly instead. "Better?"

She gave an adamant shake of her head. "No."

He didn't move. "It was my fault, you know. You're wonderful. Sexy as hell. I was going along just fine, prepared to see to you first as any gentleman would do, then you gave that provoking little moan and I lost it. Kaboom. Control blown all to hell. You should be slapping my face. You should be cursing me. I'm a pig and a lousy lover and I made promises I didn't keep."

Her head turned on the pillow and she stared toward him. Though Cary knew that without her glasses she couldn't see him, her expression of incredulous disbelief was plain to see. "That's nonsense."

He smothered a laugh. "Please tell me you don't think I'm always such a selfish ass."

Her brows came down in a frown. "You were wonderful."

Cary slid his hand a little lower on her belly, until she caught her breath. His fingertips just touched her triangle of hair. "Wonderfully selfish." And in a huskier tone, "I got inside you and you were so tight, so hot and wet, I became an animal."

She bit her lip. "I . . . I liked it."

"Yeah?" He grinned. "Me, too, obviously. But there's a lot more to this whole lovemaking business." When she remained curiously silent, he grew blunt. "You didn't come."

She caught her bottom lip in her teeth. "It, um, felt so good that I wasn't sure."

Damn, she was adorable. "You'll know when it happens, Nora. I promise." She frowned in doubt, which challenged him. "Let me prove it to you."

Sensual interest darkened her eyes as the seconds ticked by. "How?"

God, he loved her. Now and forever, the kind of love that wouldn't ever go away. And he'd just blown it in the sack. The irony was that women he'd merely liked had claimed him an excellent lover, while the woman he wanted most in his life had demolished his finesse, reducing him to a sex-crazed lunatic. He almost groaned again, but instead he sucked it up like a man and set out to make things right.

"Like this." He covered her with his palm and began to gently finger her. She was so hot, and wet. *Very wet.* Which meant he was quickly growing hard again. He would not be a pig this time. Never again. But she moaned, and that small sound tested him. He supposed it was his love for her that made everything with her sharper-edged, so acute that he could barely contain himself.

Because she looked embarrassed he leaned over her and covered her mouth with his own, muffling her sounds of pleasure. At first, he kept the pressure light, the rhythm uneven, letting her orgasm build up again. When her kisses grew bolder, almost desperate, he moved down to her breasts. The dual assault would be sweet, and would help guarantee his odds.

At the same time that he closed his mouth hotly over her nipple, he pressed two fingers deep inside her, stretching her, exacerbating already sensitive nerve endings. Her cries grew more harsh, raw. Using his thumb with devastating effect, Cary stroked her clitoris in small, circular movements that had her groaning and writhing. He kept himself in check with ruthless determination. He could feel the heat pulsing off her, the spiciness of her aroused scent—and she broke.

With a long, ragged moan, her legs stiffened, her hips jerked. He raised up to watch her, seeing the vague understanding in her dark eyes, the rush of heightened color in her face and throat. "Perfect," he whispered, keeping the pleasure steady, ensuring she got everything this time.

By small degrees, she quieted and her legs went lax, naturally sprawling. He wanted to fuck her again; he wanted to hold her to his heart and tell her everything he was feeling. He wanted so much, he honestly didn't know where to start. He should take it easy, play it by ear, wait and see what Nora thought. Yeah, that's what he'd do. He'd be patient for once. He'd keep control.

And he wouldn't make any more boneheaded moves.

Chapter Four

Awareness slowly seeped in on Nora. She felt euphoric. Weak and elated and . . . *satisfied*. Every sense was magnified. She was intensely aware of the cool air on her skin, the rumpled sheets beneath her, the incredible man making a dent in her mattress.

She smiled, so secretly pleased that she had to fight not to laugh out loud. Wow. No wonder everyone did this with such great regularity.

She felt that, at this particular moment in time, new doors had just opened for her. The whole world looked different. She'd never been the type to sleep around, to take a lover. But Cary had just changed all that, and she was so glad.

She turned her head to see him, but without her glasses, he was no more than a blur. As if he'd read her mind, he rolled to his back, did some reaching, and then her glasses were slipped onto her nose. She straightened them and took in his expression, anxious to see if he'd been as affected as she was by the sex.

His warm, mellow gaze filled with tenderness.

Relieved, Nora whispered, "Thank you."

He looked at her mouth.

"For the glasses, and the . . . the . . ."

"Orgasm?" The right side of his mouth kicked up. "Now that was my pleasure."

She matched his grin. "And mine." She pondered how to tell him that she wanted more, that she wanted to do it again, maybe not right this moment, but soon. She put a hand on his chest. "Cary," she said hesitantly.

And he blurted, "Marry me."

Her gaze snapped up and locked onto his. He looked more surprised than she felt. In fact, he appeared floored that those words had come from his mouth. Or had they? "What did you say?"

He actually flushed. Then he scowled. "You heard me."

"I'm not sure I did."

His shoulders bunched. He seemed annoyed with himself, and she could imagine why. Oh God, she'd burdened him with all her leftover dreams for marriage and children, and now he felt obligated.

"I asked if you'd marry me."

Actually, he'd just sort of demanded it, and in fact he still seemed rather combative about the offering. "Cary, you don't need to do that."

His frown sharpened, as did his annoyance. "That?"

"Propose. I mean, I was just thinking that I like it like this."

"This?"

Worse and worse. He'd barely squeezed that word out between his teeth. "Yes, with us as . . . lovers. No commitment, no responsibility." She stroked his chest. "Just pleasure."

"You said you wanted marriage," he accused, and his cheekbones were red, his green eyes incandescent with anger.

"Yes, I know, but . . . not with you."

He bolted upright in the bed. "Not. With. Me?"

Nora wanted to pull out her own tongue. How insulting that had sounded! "What I mean is—"

A distant ringing sounded and they both paused, alert. Working in the medical field, a phone was never ignored.

Cary cursed luridly. "Goddammit, that's my cell phone. I left it on your patio." Buck naked, he clambered out of her bed, out of her bedroom, and quite possibly right out of her life.

Dolt. Idiot. How could she have said such a ridiculous, mean, nasty thing to him? She knew what she meant—that she was happy having him any way she could. That making love with him was a worthwhile trade-off for marriage. That she loved him enough, she'd take what he was comfortable offering—which plainly wasn't marriage.

Stewing in bed wouldn't do her one bit of good. What if he left without even telling her good-bye? That galvanized her into action and

Nora was out of the bed in a flash. She was stepping into panties when Cary stomped back in.

He drew up short at the sight of her, with her underwear around her knees, her upper body still bare. His gaze darted here and there, lingering on her breasts and belly.

He was fully dressed, darn it. Well, except for his boxers, which were wadded up and wet on her floor. Drawn back to her senses, Nora tugged her panties up the rest of the way and crossed her arms over her breasts.

As if that broke the spell, Cary gave up his scrutiny of her body. He didn't look at her face. He stayed busy tucking in his shirt, buckling his belt. "I have to go," he said in one of the flattest tones she'd ever heard from him. "One of my patients is having trouble breathing. Probably bronchitis from the sounds of it. But she's older and afraid of most doctors, so I'm going to meet her and her son at the emergency room."

He was such a remarkable, caring man and all she could do was stand there in nothing more than panties, wracking her brain for something to say. "Cary . . ."

He shot her a quick, insincere smile. "We can talk later. Duty calls." He hesitated, then took one long step toward her, put a perfunctory peck on her forehead, and rushed from the room.

Nora sank to the edge of the bed. It was badly mussed, the pillows off on the floor, the sheets trailing over the side. The scent of their lovemaking still lingered in the air, and stupidly, tears prickled her eyes. She was a complete and inexcusable social hazard.

He hadn't promised to call, but he had said they'd talk. Later. Whatever that might mean. She pinned all her hopes on it because if he called, then she could explain.

With nothing left to do, Nora dragged herself into the shower. She still felt weak in the knees, and places she'd barely paid attention to before were now achy.

By eleven o'clock that night, she gave up staring at a silent phone and tried to sleep, but she couldn't put Cary from her mind. She missed him already. She wanted him again. It was almost dawn before she got any rest.

The weekend continued in a heat wave, frazzling her nerves, making her listless. Liza called and wanted to go shopping, but Nora turned her down. She was afraid to leave for fear she'd miss his call. Like a lovesick teenager, she carried the phone with her everywhere, out to the pool, while doing yard work. By Sunday morning, when Cary still hadn't called, she got angry.

How did a man make love to a woman and then just walk away? But she knew it happened all the time, which was one of the reasons she'd avoided affairs. Sex was just sex and these days didn't necessarily imply more.

But this time . . . She covered her face with her hands. He'd asked her to marry him and she'd shot him down. What if that was the only reason he didn't call?

When the phone rang, her heart almost stopped. She stood there through four rings, immobilized by hope before ungluing her feet and racing to snatch it up.

"Hello?"

"Hey, it's Liza. I'm bored. If you don't want to shop, let's do lunch."

Disappointment staggered Nora. "Oh, it's you."

Feigning insult, Liza said, "Gee thanks."

Nora thumped her hand against her forehead. Now she was insulting her friend, too! "I'm sorry. I really am. And yeah, sure, lunch sounds great." She desperately needed a distraction.

"So much enthusiasm." Liza laughed. "I have a better idea. Why don't you tell me who you were hoping to hear from?"

Why not? Maybe Liza could give her some advice. "A hound dog."

"Do tell! A sexy, doctor-type hound dog? Catch me up on what I've missed."

Nora strode to the couch, collapsed onto it, and in practically one breath rattled off her tale of woe.

To her surprise, Liza cackled like a crazed hen.

Bemused by that reaction, Nora explained, "It's really not a humorous story."

"Oh, honey, of course it is. Women don't wait around for men to call anymore. They pick up a phone and do the deed themselves."

The mere thought had Nora wincing. "Oh no. I couldn't."

"Not even to apologize—which you owe him, by the way? If he doesn't want to hear it, or it seems he doesn't care, then you have your answer. It's better than stewing, isn't it?"

Stewing and moping and wallowing in her

misery . . . "I suppose." And then, reluctantly, "Maybe after you and I finish lunch—"

"No way. Forget that. I say call him now. Or better yet, just drop in on him. And don't say you can't, because he dropped in on you, right? Turnabout is fair play."

Nora sank lower on the couch. "You really think it'd be all right to do that?"

"I'm betting he'll be thrilled to see you. But hey, nothing ventured, nothing gained."

Nora wished she had Liza's confidence. She drew a long breath for courage, and said, "All right, I'll do it."

"That'a girl. And one more thing."

"Yes?"

"You damn sure better call me later tonight and tell me all the nitty-gritty details!"

"I promise." For the first time since she'd misspoken to Cary, Nora was smiling. She glanced at the clock. It was nearing noon and she hadn't bothered to do more than dress, but now she felt like a woman with a mission. She headed to the bathroom for a cool shower, a touch of makeup, and a dab of perfume.

Within half an hour, she'd donned one of her prettiest sundresses, had her hair and makeup just right, and was on her way to Cary's. He wasn't far from her home, something she considered fortunate given her nervousness. Given any time to reconsider, she was likely to turn back around.

Unlike her, Cary had chosen a condo over a house. She parked in his private drive, and before she could chicken out, she trotted up the walkway and rang his doorbell.

No one answered.

With a feeling of déjà vu, she cautiously, hopefully made her way around back. His was a corner condo, secluded by thick hedges on one side and a privacy fence on the other. There was no pool in his small patch of backyard, but maybe he was grilling. Or just sunning himself.

Nora was several feet away when she recognized Cary's voice barking, "I don't want her, Axel, so shut the hell up."

Nora staggered to a halt while her heart sank into her feet. He didn't want her?

Another voice, not Axel's or Cary's, said calmly, "Keep your voice down. And Axel, leave him alone. Can't you see he's suffering?"

"I am not suffering," Cary growled.

"You're lovesick," that other voice insisted, "but too stubborn to admit it."

"Exactly," Axel said. "But Patti could cure you of that if you'd just give her a chance. If she's anything like her friend, and I think she is, she'll have you moaning with pleasure instead of sorrow. Guaranteed."

Cary said, "Booker, I'm going to break his teeth, I swear, if he mentions Patti again."

Patti? Who the heck was Patti?

"Well, what the hell do you want me to do?" Axel suddenly demanded. "I told you not to screw with my office dynamics. I told you Nora wasn't your type. But do you ever listen to me? No. You even go and propose to her, damn it."

"It was a bonehead move, I admit," Cary said. And then he murmured, more to himself than anyone else, "And I'd promised myself I wasn't going to make any more bonehead moves."

"So now you're sitting here looking like a wolf who got caught in a trap and had to chew his own foot off."

There was a startled moment of silence after that awesomely descriptive analogy, then Booker laughed. "He's not like a self-maimed wolf at all. He's just in love."

In love? With her? Nora hoped so.

"Jesus," Cary complained, "you're both like old women. Can't a man have some peace?"

Booker said, "Not when he's in love."

"I'm going to call her," Axel stated. "I'll ask her just what the hell is wrong with you—no, Cary, I mean it. I can straighten this out—no, let go."

Nora heard a scuffle, a couple of dull thuds, and she hurried around the privacy fence. Axel, shirtless and in shorts, was on his back, gripping a cell phone for dear life while Cary, in shorts and a T-shirt, had him in a headlock, choking him and struggling to pry the phone loose.

Beside them, arms crossed and smiling as if he didn't have a care in the world, was the man she assumed to be Booker. Nora had never met him, only knew his name because she'd just heard it, but he looked a lot like Axel.

He noticed her and raised a brow. "Can I help you?"

Both Cary and Axel paused in their physical debate to swivel their heads toward her.

"Nora!"

Axel took swift advantage of her presence.

"What the hell is wrong—" Cary's hand clamped over his mouth. It wasn't an easy thing, holding Axel down. He was thicker, more muscular than Cary.

She looked at all three men and felt like she'd fallen into the rabbit hole. "Um . . . what are you doing?"

Axel thrashed about, mumbling urgently from behind Cary's hand. Cary scowled and pressed a knee into his ribs. "Nothing."

Booker grinned. "Typical male bonding stuff. That's all." He stepped over the fallen men and held out his hand. "I'm Booker, Axel's brother and Cary's friend by association. You're really Nora?"

"Yes." She shook his hand—then found out he wouldn't let go.

"You're here to see Cary?"

"Yes." Nervously, she glanced toward Cary and Axel. They were no longer struggling, but neither were they getting up. She cleared her throat. "I'm sorry to intrude . . ."

Cary scowled. "You were eavesdropping, weren't you?"

"Yes."

He shoved to his feet, managing to kick Axel twice on his way up. "Say something besides yes, damn it."

Nora lifted her chin. "All right. I did eavesdrop but you did it first. And stop cursing at me. And while I'm at it, you look like an idiot rolling around on the ground."

That startled Cary, and he grinned—until he

noticed Booker still had her hand. "What the hell are you doing, Booker?" He strode forward. "Turn her loose."

Now that he was free, Axel bounded up. "Why don't you want to marry Cary? Hell, he's a good catch. All the women want him."

Nora blinked while watching Cary's face go blank. His left eye twitched, then he jerked around with a snarl, but Booker caught him before he could reach Axel.

To avoid more physical conflict, Nora rushed to answer. "I don't want him to feel coerced."

"Why would he feel coerced?" Booker asked.

"Because I told him I wanted to get married."

"But not to *me.*" Cary looked very aggressive again, making her frown.

"You didn't give me a chance to explain."

"Explain now," Axel suggested. He was busy dusting himself off, so he didn't see Cary reach for him. He got shoved a good two feet and barely stayed upright. "What?" Axel said. "I'm curious, too, you know."

Nora couldn't help it—she laughed. When all three men stared at her, she laughed some more. Misunderstanding, Cary started to turn away, but she caught his arm, pulled him around, and hugged him tight. "I'm sorry. But it's funny, seeing grown men, doctors, grappling like little boys."

Cary stood frozen for only a moment before his arms came around her. With his mouth touching her ear, he whispered, "That's all most men are—little boys at heart."

"I love you."

Cary froze again. He started to push her back so he could see her face, but Nora held on.

Behind them, Axel whispered, "What'd she say?"

And Booker replied, "Shh."

"You love me?"

Nora nodded against his chest. "And I want to marry you, too, if the offer still stands."

"Why'd you tell me no the first time then? Not to belabor the point, but I'd never proposed before. It sort of took it out of me."

"I'm sorry. I didn't want you to feel that you had to marry me just because we . . . you know."

She could hear the grin in his voice when he whispered, "Sex had nothing to do with it. Especially considering I blew it."

"You did not!"

Axel said, "What's that?"

Cary turned to him with a scowl. "Booker, if you want your brother alive and well, you better drag him out of here."

Booker chuckled. "Promise to invite us to the wedding and we'll both go."

"Yeah, sure, whatever."

"I had to leave anyway," Axel announced. "All things considered, Patti's probably out of the question."

Nora flashed him an angry look. "She's *definitely* out."

"That's what I figured. So I better go, uh, let her down easy." He winked, and together he and Booker went through the house. Seconds later, Cary and Nora heard the front door close.

Cary turned back to her, and this time Nora could see the love in his beautiful green eyes. She laughed again and squeezed him tighter. "I've been in love with you for months. Thank you for not giving up on me."

"You were more than worth the chase, Nora." He tilted her back. "Now, about my substandard performance Friday."

"You were wonderful," she insisted yet again.

"Care to give me another shot at proving how wonderful *we* can be? Like . . . right now maybe?"

Her heart started racing at just the suggestion. "Yes."

"I'll wear a rubber this time."

Nora smiled. "I doubt one time will do the deed, but you did say you wanted children."

Cary bent to kiss her, long and slow and deep. "With you, honey, I want everything."

So happy she felt ready to burst, Nora cupped his face and sighed. "With me, you have it."

PLAYING DOCTOR

Chapter One

Trying to be inconspicuous, Libby Preston glanced over her shoulder—and found that sexy, dark brown gaze still following her every move. He had a way of looking that felt like touching. Warm and gentle, but bold. Brazen, but complimentary.

She wanted to fan herself, but that'd be giving too much away, so instead she pretended not to notice and continued setting out more food on the buffet table.

They'd been at the stupid party for hours now and he'd done little more than watch her, smiling occasionally, giving her that sensual once-over that made chills race up her arms. He was a devil all right, and very sexy. She'd be smart to steer clear of him.

But really, what choice did she even have? Doctors and not-quite nurses didn't mix very often. Her uncle hadn't given her the job of playing waitress for his party so that she could flirt. No, it was one more way to pay him back for all she owed him, and she'd do well to remember that. And to remember her place: a lowly nobody among esteemed physicians.

The man eating her up with his eyes probably thought her part of the catering crew. And that suited her fine.

Whatever he thought, he kept her keenly aware of him. Anytime she looked up, he was looking back, even while speaking with others, even while asking for a drink or munching on the fancy snacks.

Unlike the other docs attending the benefit, he didn't wear a tie. Or a jacket. He'd unbuttoned his silky, coffee-colored dress shirt at the throat, showing a sprinkling of dark chest hair that intrigued her. He had his sleeves rolled up, and she couldn't help but notice the thickness of his wrists, the size of his capable hands, and more black hair on his forearms. The shirt tucked into black dress slacks, emphasizing the contrast of his wide shoulders against a flat abdomen and trim hips.

Restless fingers had rumpled his midnight black hair, and beard shadow colored his jaw. He was unlike any other man in the room.

He was unlike any man she'd ever seen.

More than one woman had noticed him. But

strangely enough, he paid little attention to the finely dressed female physicians flirting with him, vying for his attention. Instead, he leaned against the wall, at his leisure, sipping his drink and . . . watching her.

Whoa. Libby pulled herself together and finished emptying her tray of hors d'oeuvres on the linen-covered table. Giving the man her back, she retreated to the kitchen.

Her uncle stood in idle conversation with a touted surgeon. As the chief of staff at their local hospital, he knew everyone. Uncle Elwood could give her the name of the man—but no, she wouldn't ask. Not only would it be unforgivable to interrupt, but questions about doctors would only earn her a lecture.

When her mother died, Uncle Elwood had grudgingly taken her in, but he made a point of reminding her that if his sister hadn't been such a frivolous partier, she'd have been the one to raise Libby instead of foisting her off on him. In his eyes, the apple didn't fall far from the tree. He often claimed Libby was the exact image of his sister, in looks and temperament. Therefore, at least in his mind, she could be no different.

Libby knew she had a lot to prove to her uncle. And she would—then she'd leave his life with a big fat *thank you*, owing him nothing, not a dime, not gratitude, nada, zip.

With everything currently in order, Libby helped herself to a small glass of punch. She'd just gotten the icy drink to her lips when Uncle Elwood harrumphed behind her.

Wincing, Libby turned, raising one eyebrow in inquiry.

"The sun has long set and you haven't yet lit the torches along the garden path."

"Oh." Libby glanced out the enormous window behind the kitchen sink. "Yeah, I'll get right on that." She upended her glass and guzzled down the spiked punch in one long gulp, then covered her mouth with a hand to muffle her delicate burp.

Much aggrieved, her uncle sighed. "Please try to behave yourself, Libby. These are my esteemed colleagues. As chief of staff at the hospital, they expect much decorum from me. You mustn't—"

Well used to the lectures, Libby cut him off by patting the front of his rich suit jacket. "I won't shame you, Uncle Elwood, have no fear." She set her glass in the sink and dug in the drawer for matches. "What do I do after I light the torches?"

As if hoping to think of something more, he glanced around, but as Libby already knew, organization ruled. "I suppose you could circulate, make sure everyone has a fresh drink, that the buffet table stays full, things of that nature."

Sounded to Libby like she'd be twiddling her thumbs a lot. She winked at Uncle Elwood. "Sure thing." Waving the box of matches in the air, she headed out of the kitchen. "I'll go take care of the gardens right now."

At mid-April, the evenings remained too cool for most people to venture out, but she wouldn't mind the breath of fresh air. The stuffy nabobs her uncle deemed friends were enough to cur-

dle her blood. She'd been hustling for hours
and had worked up a dewy sweat. With any luck,
she could linger outdoors and catch a breather,
with no one the wiser.

The second she reentered the room, Mr. Sexy
Brown Eyes tracked her, following as she crossed
the room to the double sliding doors. Libby did
her utmost to stay impervious. Since her mother's
death right before her fifteenth birthday, there'd
been no time in her life for guys. Until she became a full-fledged nurse and gained financial
and emotional independence from her uncle,
nothing would change.

She could wish it different, but for tonight at
least, Brown Eyes would just have to entertain
himself.

With an indulgent smile, Axel Dean watched
the young lady exit the room of suffocating,
overbearing people. Damn, she was sweet on
the eyes. Tall, nearly as tall as he was, with raven
black hair and piercing blue eyes and an air of
negligence that dared him, calling on his baser
instincts, stripping away the façade of civility he
tried to don in polite company.

Her straight hair skimmed her shoulders,
darker than his own, blue black without a single
hint of red. It was so silky it looked fluid, moving
when she moved, shimmering with highlights
from the glow of candles. The white catering
shirt and black slacks didn't do much for her
figure, which he guessed to be slim and toned.

She didn't have the lush curves he usually fa-
vored, but what she lacked in body she made up
for in attitude.

And attitude, as he well knew, made a huge
difference in bed.

As a waiter passed, Axel plunked his empty
glass down onto the tray and headed for the
sliding doors. He hated uptight, formal affairs,
but being a doctor often obligated him to attend. That didn't mean he had to linger. That
didn't mean he had to mingle.

Especially when more enlivening entertain-
ment waited outside.

Making certain no one paid him any mind,
he slipped through the doors and onto a wide
balcony lit by twinkle lights that mirrored the
stars in the evening sky. He waited, saying a
silent prayer that no one followed him. Every
time he attended a gathering, women hit on
him. And that'd be okay, fine and dandy by him,
given that he adored women, but not within his
professional circle.

He absolutely never, ever, dated anyone in his
field. Not even anyone related to someone in
his field.

Despite the marital bliss of both his brother
and his best friend, he had no intention of set-
tling down any time soon. That being the case,
it wouldn't be wise to get involved with relatives,
friends, or associates of the people he worked
with. Walking away could cause a scene, and
then the entire situation would get sticky and
uncomfortable.

There were plenty of women who weren't interested in medicine, like secretaries, lawyers . . . or caterers.

He'd been prepared to be bored spitless tonight. Then he'd seen her hustling around the crowded room with robust energy. At first he'd assumed her to be a mere waitress for the catering company, but given how she performed each and every job, from putting out food to collecting empty dishes to directing the others, she might actually be the one in charge. Given her air of command and confidence, he figured her to be late twenties, maybe early thirties. Sexy. Mature. Flirtatious.

His heartbeat sped up, just imagining how the night might end.

When no one followed, Axel went down the curving wooden stairs to the garden paths behind Elwood's home. The pompous ass loved to flaunt his money, and why not? He had plenty to flaunt.

Spring had brought a profusion of blooming flowers to fill the air with heady scents. The chilly evening breeze didn't faze Axel as he searched the darkness for her. Then he saw a flare of light, realized it was a match, and made his way silently toward her.

She had her back to him, going on tiptoe to reach the top of an ornate torch anchored to the ground and surrounded by evergreens. Just as the wick caught, Axel said, "Hello."

She went perfectly still, poised on tiptoes, arms reaching up to the top of the torch. Slowly, in an oh-so-aware way, she relaxed and turned to face him.

Insufficient moonlight left long shadows everywhere, and with the torch behind her, silhouetting her frame, Axel couldn't read her features.

She cleared her throat. "You're not enjoying the party."

A statement, not a question. He put his hands in his pockets, his mood already improved. "I never do."

"Then why attend?"

He took one step closer to her and reached for her hand. Her fingers were chilled and felt very small in his light grip. He shrugged one shoulder. "You never know when something'll happen to make it worthwhile." Using his thumb, he stroked her knuckles. "Like this."

"This?"

She didn't pull away, but wariness had entered her husky tone, cautioning him to go slowly. "You're a smart woman. You feel it."

Her teeth shone briefly in a quick smile. "What I've felt is you watching me."

"Mmmm. Watching—and wishing." He tugged her a bit closer. "Wishing for a private moment, just like this."

Sexual tension hung in the air between them. Axel counted the heavy beats of his heart, tried to judge her response . . .

She turned away, saying lightly, "I have other torches to light." Her hand remained held in his.

"I'll keep you company." Axel followed along,

trailing her as she wove her way into the gardens. Elwood owned ten acres, all of it wooded but meticulously manicured. The acreage closest to his home was especially lush with ornate landscaping.

"The path leads down to the pond," she explained. "It's not a quick jaunt."

Filling his words with innuendo, Axel murmured, "Quick is overrated. I prefer going slow." The scent of her heated skin carried back to him on the breeze, more delectable than the sweet fragrance of the flowers. He breathed deeply, and his gut clenched with need.

She made a sound that could have been a chuckle or exasperation. "It's deeper into the woods."

Grinning to himself, Axel growled, "I can go deep."

Now *that* was a laugh. She glanced over her shoulder, eyes twinkling, white teeth showing in a grin. "I meant that there might be mosquitoes."

"It's too early in the season." His thumb pressed her palm. "The bugs won't be biting— but I might."

Another husky chuckle, then: "You're pretty outrageous, you know that?"

He loved the sound of her voice, playful and not at all shy. "Just trying to make headway with a beautiful woman."

"Trying for a one-night stand, you mean."

His fingers tightened on hers, pulling her to a halt beside a gurgling fountain of marble nymphs, flanked by benches and a profusion of flowers. Small colored lights within the fountain sent a rainbow of subtle color to dance in the air.

She stared at him, her gaze level, even challenging.

Lifting a hand, Axel touched the cool velvet of her cheek, trailed his fingers into the warmer silk of her hair. Damn, but he loved how women felt, and he especially loved the feel of this particular woman. "Is that a problem?"

Her lips parted. Her eyes almost closed. Then she snapped them open and cleared her throat. "You are a temptation. But if I succumbed—the key word being *if*—then no, one night is all I could spare, believe me."

The way she said that . . . "You're married?" God, he hoped not. His disappointment at the thought was extreme, far too exaggerated for the brief time he'd known her. He didn't confine himself to many rules, but dallying with married broads headed his personal list of taboos.

"Hardly."

She made it sound as if marriage were a heinous act, a sentiment he shared. He used both hands to cup her face. Her softness seemed addictive, sending his mind into a tailspin of erotic images, making him wonder just how soft she might be in other, more carnal places.

Those thoughts brought about a semi-erection, urging him to clear the way, and quickly. "Engaged then?" *Let her say no.*

She licked her lips. "No."

Thank God. He eased her closer, and it struck him how well she fit his body, her height aligning her mouth just below his, her belly to his groin, her slender thighs bumping his thicker, more muscular legs.

They had traveled enough distance from the house that no one could possibly see them. He stared at her mouth, and could almost taste her.

Her hand flattened on his chest just over his heart. "Not so fast, Romeo. What about you?"

"What about me?"

"Involved?"

"No." And with more vehemence, "Hell no. Not married, not engaged, and definitely not looking to be either."

Seconds ticked by while she stared at him, and Axel prayed she'd come to an agreeable conclusion.

Finally, on a long sigh, she said, "I think I have to kiss you. I'll never forgive myself if I don't."

Something tightened inside him—anticipation. Something loosened at the same time—relief.

He tilted up her chin. "We can't have you berating yourself later, now can we?" His mouth curled in a smile of welcome. She wanted to kiss him? Then by all means, he'd make it easy on her. "Make it any kind of kiss you want. Just make it soon, before I forget my manners and take charge."

She snorted. "I doubt you have any manners, but with an invitation like that . . ." Still holding the box of matches, she braced her hands on his shoulders and leaned in. Her nose touched his, playfully nuzzled him while her warm breath teased his mouth and her breasts just barely skimmed his chest.

And then her lips were on him, scalding hot, damp, so sweet that he actually groaned out loud.

She eased back with a smile. "What was that?"

Axel caught her waist—a damn narrow waist—and brought her back in close again. His breath was labored, his boner now full-fledged and throbbing. "Lust, darlin'. Pure, unadulterated lust." His voice dropped to a husky growl, and he ordered, "Now kiss me again."

Chapter Two

Instead of obeying, her fingers covered his mouth. "I don't know," she fretted. "This feels very dangerous."

"So live dangerously." Axel nipped the tip of her finger, sucked it into the warmth of his mouth, and her lips parted on a whispered, *"Oh."*

Satisfaction roared through him. He licked the center of her palm and rumbled, "Better yet, I'll kiss you." He didn't give her time to think about it or to deny him. He took her mouth with the verve of a sexually starved man, when in fact he never stayed celibate for more than a week. But somehow, this felt different. Hotter, more exciting.

He had to have her. No other option would do.

Her lips parted to the prod of his tongue and he sank in, tasting her deeply, slanting his head and bending her back so she'd feel his power, his greed. This time she groaned. The box of matches hit the ground with a quiet rustle and her nails sank into his shoulders, giving him a quick thrill that burned down to the core of his masculine being.

Usually, he calculated his every move, timing himself for the best reaction, aware of the woman's every response and countering it in a way to ensure success. This time, he acted solely on instinct and his own escalating need. Before he had time to consider it, his hand was over her breast, carefully because she felt so small and delicate, so completely female. She might have gasped, but with his tongue in her mouth, their breath soughing together, it was hard to tell.

With his free arm around her back, he arched her into his body, holding her snug, pressing his dick into the soft seam of her thighs. Oh yeah, that felt good, too good.

She pulled her mouth free, dropping her head back on a shuddering moan.

Axel looked at her, the moonlight playing over her face, her lashes sending long feathery shadows over her cheeks. She looked young and aroused and ripe.

He stared down at the sight of his dark hand covering her chest over the white shirt. Her heartbeat galloped and heat poured off, filling his nose with feminine spice.

He bent his head to her throat, deliberately sucking her skin in against his teeth to mark her while plucking her buttons open, one by one, all the way to the waistband of her black slacks.

Both her hands sank into his hair. "This is insane," she all but wailed—but she didn't shove him away.

With her shirt gaping open, Axel slipped his hand inside, under her bra, and cupped silky bare flesh.

Their gazes met and held.

Her stiff little nipple prodded his palm.

Keeping her eyes locked with his, Axel pushed the material aside, easing her shirt over her shoulder and down her arm, tugging the lacy bra low. He captured her nipple between fingers and thumb, and tugged.

A near silent moan shuddered past her parted lips and her lashes fluttered.

Neither of them said a word. The fountain gurgled, music floated on the air from the live band at the party, leaves rustled, and crickets chirped. All Axel could hear was the rushing of blood in his ears and his own resounding heartbeat.

His attention dipped to her breast. Beautiful. Small, but round and firm, and her nipple looked darkly flushed in the dim light. Her pale flesh made a striking contrast to her inky black hair. He pictured her white thighs open, the black curls between, and wanted her now, right here in the gardens.

His arm around her waist pressed her upward an inch, and he bent to suck her nipple into his mouth.

"Oh God." She half laughed, half groaned, then whispered in amazement, "What *am* I doing?"

"We're having fun." He insinuated his leg between hers, immobilizing her. "And we've only just started."

"But—"

He sucked her nipple again, effectively cutting off her breath and ending whatever protestations she might have made. And while she was quiet . . . He smoothed his hand down her ribs, over the slight, delectable roundness of her belly, and pressed it between her legs.

She jumped in surprise. "Oh wow."

Axel could feel the heat of her through her slacks. "Why couldn't you be wearing a skirt?" he complained. He lifted his head and smiled at her while gently stroking, petting. His voice dark and low, he teased, "I'd much rather be touching you instead of stiff cotton."

She hung in his grasp, panting, flushed and ready, and then she whispered, "They unzip."

His knees nearly gave out. If ever permission had been granted, that was it. Scooping her up, Axel took three steps to a marble bench, stopping in front of it and standing her back on her feet. When she swayed, he caught her, steadying her then seating himself in front of her.

"Let's take care of the rest of these buttons first." In rapid order he pulled her shirt free of her pants, opened the last button, and dropped the shirt to the ground. One side of her bra was down, showing her breast. He expertly opened the front clasp and the cups parted.

A small sound escaped her, and again she swayed.

"Beautiful." He could have looked at her for

hours, but now wasn't the time, not with a party going on behind them and his dick so hard he hurt with needing her.

When she started to cover herself, Axel caught her hands and put them on his shoulders. "Hold on to me."

Again, her short nails bit into his flesh, proving that she felt some of the same urgency that gripped him. To ease her into things, Axel forced himself to be content with her breasts for a time, sucking, licking, going from one nipple to the other.

When she trembled all over, he opened the top button of her slacks.

She kept squirming, making all those soft female sounds guaranteed to drive a man into a frenzy. He dragged the zipper down, and finally her slacks opened over a pale belly. Without hesitation, Axel tugged the pants down her hips, all the way to her knees.

She gasped, stumbling back out of reach.

Axel stared up at her. "Come back here."

Hands folded around her middle, she made an enticing, adorable picture. Her knees peeked at him above the lowered waistband of her slacks. Her open bra framed her modest breasts and tightly puckered nipples. Moonlight glowed on her startled face, showing her uncertainty and the arousal she couldn't hide.

"You don't have to be afraid," Axel soothed. "I know this is fast. Mach speed fast. And believe me, I'm not in the habit of fucking in the garden."

Her mouth firmed at his crude language.

"Still, you can call a halt at any time."

She watched him, keeping a scant distance that wouldn't do her any good at all if he were the type to force a woman, which he wasn't.

"You'd stop right now?"

It'd kill him, but . . . "If you said stop, of course I would." He waited, but she kept quiet, relieving him and firing him at the same time. "You should know, from the moment I saw you, I wanted you. Deny it if you have to, but I think you felt the same."

Again he waited, giving her time to adjust, and little by little her shoulders relaxed.

She bit her lip, then said, "This is so strange."

"But exciting?"

"Yes."

Axel couldn't keep his gaze on her face, not with her body almost bare. He alternated between perusing her breasts, her belly, her thighs, and those incredible blue eyes filled with turmoil. "If you come over here," he promised, "I'll kiss you again. Everywhere."

She briefly closed her eyes, fighting some internal battle, before searching his face in the darkness. "Everywhere?"

His chest labored. "Yeah." Saying it made him feel it, the texture of her flesh on his tongue, the richer scent of her in private places. His nostrils flared, his muscles clenched. "Your mouth," he told her. "Your nipples. Your belly." He reached out one long arm and hooked his fingers in the top of her slacks between her knees. "If you let me get your panties down, I'll kiss you there, too, until you can't stand it any-more."

Breathing hard, she allowed herself to be tugged forward.

"You'd like that," Axel told her in a coaxing whisper. He wrapped his arms around her ass and nuzzled her soft belly, inching his lips lower, to the front of her lace undies. "Right here." His tongue pressed, and he could barely taste her through the lace.

Her knees threatened to give out, which was answer enough for Axel. Almost.

She seemed so timid that his oft nonexistent conscience prickled. He pulled her into his lap and kissed her again, long and deep until she went limp, then began clutching at him. Finally, when her reserves had been stripped away, he said, "Sorry to press you, but I need to know you're okay with this. I need to know you won't have regrets."

Her soft sigh thrilled him, as did the quiet, "No regrets," that she murmured against his mouth.

Heart pounding, Axel looked at her body curled on his lap. Her breasts were entirely bare. Her belly trembled with each shallow, fast breath. And when he slipped his hand into her panties, her thighs opened without his instruc-tion.

Soft, springy curls tangled around his fingers. He simply cupped her, not moving, giving her time to get used to that. She turned her face into his chest and tenderness rolled over him, taking him by surprise.

It suddenly dawned on him that she could be risking her job with the catering company, that she could end up humiliated if they got caught.

He glanced up at the house, and presumed they weren't missed. No one hovered on the deck, searching through the darkness for them. Through the glass doors and windows, he watched people milling around and he could hear the drone of conversation mingled with music. She'd only lit a few torches before he'd distracted her, leaving the grounds dark enough to conceal them.

He kissed the top of her head, down to her ear. "Give me your mouth."

She lifted her face and he covered her lips in a long, soft, deep, eating kiss. She clung to him, kissing him back, taking his tongue and sucking on it. And when her hips lifted, silently urging him on, he parted her gently and pressed one finger in, encountering wet heat that sent his heart into a race.

Growling, he deepened the kiss even more. Insane, wanting a woman so much when he didn't even know her name. But now wasn't the time to ask. No way in hell would he interrupt the moment.

She was so damn small and tight, squeezing his finger while little purring sounds escaped her and she squirmed on his lap.

Axel pulled out, then inserted another finger, amazed that he was actually stretching her and that she groaned in excitement even as she stilled in discomfort.

"Easy," he whispered, a little awed, a little over-whelmed. "Am I hurting you?"

"Don't talk," she said. "Please."

He should have been offended, but at the moment he just didn't give a damn. He kissed her ear, dipping his tongue inside, then licking her throat, and finally down to her breasts, suck-ling while gently fingering her, thrusting, teas-ing, taking her higher and higher.

He gauged her reaction, registering each shudder, each heated sound, the way she taut-ened, more and more and more . . .

Raising his face to watch her, he put his thumb to her clitoris. Her eyes squeezed shut and her teeth locked. He circled, rubbed, again and again.

"Oh God." Her thighs stiffened, her back arched, her face contorted, unself-conscious and real, and then she cried out, one hand knotted in the front of his shirt, the other fisted against his back.

Quickly, Axel covered her mouth with his own to muffle the sound of her unrestrained pleasure. Hips moving against his hand, body drowning in heat, she rode out the climax until finally she went utterly lax against him. If he hadn't kept a tight hold on her, she'd have poured right off his lap to the leaf-covered ground.

Axel cradled her close, hugging her, kissing her throat. He always enjoyed a woman's plea-sure, but somehow this seemed different. She was so honest in her climax, so open, that he felt . . . moved.

"Very nice," he said, shaking off the odd sensation, anxious to get inside her.

"Yeah. Nice." Then she giggled.

Smiling, Axel lifted his head. "It's funny?"

"Astounding." She drew a deep breath and let it out, dropping her head back with a groan. "Man, I had no idea. You make it seem so easy."

Somewhat lost, Axel said, "It?"

She sat up a little and smiled, touched his face. "The whole sex thing. Especially the satisfaction part."

More confused by the second, he tilted his head. "I'm not following you."

She grinned, gave him a smooching kiss, and said, "That was my first. Orgasm, I mean."

Oh. Well . . . Pride swelled his chest. "You must have been out with some bozos, then."

Shaking her head, she said, "No, actually, I meant . . . well, I shouldn't admit this. It's sort of embarrassing."

No way in hell would he let her get away with *not* telling him now. "It's dark. It's just us." He smoothed back her hair, cradled her cheek. "No secrets."

She hesitated, then finally said, "I've never been with a guy."

Oh shit.

His stomach bottomed out and his heartbeat went into double time. Like every guy everywhere, some really awesome woman-on-woman sex scenes crowded his already turned-on brain. "You mean you're a . . . ?"

"No!" She laughed, swatted at him. "I'm not gay. I meant that I'm a virgin."

His blood ran cold. No, hell no. He pulled back, appalled. "Tell me you're making that up."

"Of course I'm not." Then, with a chilling frown and a stiffened spine: "Is that a problem?"

"Uh . . ." Hell yes, it was a problem. He avoided virgins almost as much as he avoided associates. Rather than answer, he asked another question. "How old are you?"

"Twenty-one."

Dear God, he was robbing the cradle. He had sweatshirts older than her. Hell, he might even have underwear older than her.

As if she'd turned red-hot, he jerked his hands back and held them up. "I didn't realize. That is, you look older."

"What difference does it make?" She sat straight, perched on his lap, her breasts still bare, her pants still around her knees.

Oh God, oh God. "Could you, maybe . . ." Talk about awkward. "Get up?" He groaned. "And get dressed."

Clearly affronted, her chin tucked in. "You're kidding, right?"

"I wish." He couldn't believe that he, Axel Dean, sexual addict, known hedonist, had given such an order. Especially with his boner still prodding her sweet behind. His brother would laugh his ass off. Cary, his best friend, would faint from shock. But he absolutely could not do this.

The little darling on his lap didn't budge. "If this is because I'm a virgin—"

"And a baby."

"I am *not* a baby."

Proof positive right there. "You're defensive as only the young can be." He bodily lifted her from his lap and hastened to stand. His legs shook. Damn, he was horny. She'd given him a fantasy, then ripped it away with a cold dash of reality.

Women could be so cruel.

"Look," he said, starting to worry. "Let's forget this, okay? No need to tell anyone—"

"And you called me a baby?" She yanked her pants up so hard, she almost lifted herself off her feet. "You can relax, you . . . you . . . *tease.*"

"Tease!"

She zipped and buttoned with undivided fury. "I have no intention of telling anyone that I was stupid enough, gullible enough, ridiculous enough to let you touch me."

Now he started to feel offended. "Gullible?"

"Exactly. I thought you had other intentions. You misled me."

Axel leaned close. "You ungrateful brat. I made you come."

"Ha! You pulled up short, that's what you did."

Oh, now she insulted his ability. Eyes narrowed, Axel accused, "You liked it."

Nose to nose with him, she said, "Prove it." Then she sneered, "Oh wait, you're *afraid* to. Virgins terrify you."

Heat and embarrassment reddened his face. Voice wooden, he snarled, "They don't terrify me. They just complicate things."

"If I hadn't told you, you wouldn't even have known."

"Bullshit. I knew." Sorta. He had noticed how tight she was, and that awe in her face when the orgasm took her spoke volumes, but . . .

"You had no idea until I stupidly spilled my guts. And here I'd figured you for an experienced man. I thought I could have a little fun, learn a few things, then never have to see you again."

Of all the outlandish plans. "You were going to *use* me?"

"Mutual use." She sniffed as she stabbed her shirt back into the waistband of her pants. "But you had to go and ruin everything."

"Not everything," Axel told her in a haze of anger. "You still don't ever have to see me again."

"Thank God for small favors." She turned her back and bent over.

Staring at that sexy, upturned rump, Axel sucked in his breath, caught between taking her after all, and giving her a swift swat for her rudeness.

She felt around on the ground until she located the matches, then straightened. "With any luck," she yelled, starting along the path again, "you'll be long gone before I return from lighting the torches."

"You can bet I will be," Axel hollered right back. Then he realized he had yelled and drew himself up. Shit, he shouldn't be making so much noise. He glanced up at the house, but luckily he didn't see faces pressed to the glass, trying to determine the cause of the commotion.

He turned, stomping back toward the house, praying his erection would be gone before he reached it. But it was so dark out. And that stubborn little female was so small . . .

Guided by a conscience he hadn't known existed, he hung back, lingering in the shadows, watching her. He told himself he'd make sure she got back to the house safe. Yeah, it was gentlemanly concern that kept him watching her. That's all.

He sure as hell wasn't interested in a virginal post-teen.

He kept track of her as she lit each torch before stomping on to another. At the pond, she paused. Her head dropped forward and for one single instant, she covered her face, filling Axel with guilt.

Please don't let her cry, he prayed. He detested crying women.

In the next instant, she shook her fist at the sky, growled like a wild animal, and turned to plod up the path to the house.

Axel grinned despite himself. She really was in a temper, all because she wanted him. Cute.

No, scratch that.

She wasn't cute.

She was a catastrophe waiting to happen. A virgin on the loose, with experimenting on her mind. Luckily, he'd escaped her clutches in time.

Yeah, real lucky.

Shit.

He didn't bother going back to the house. El-wood wouldn't remember if he'd said good-bye or not. Axel dug his keys from his pocket and went around the house to the drive. He climbed into his BMW and slammed the door.

All the way home, he groused to himself. Even with the windows down and the cool wind in his face, he burned. He kept remembering the feel of her, how she tasted, the look on her face as she came.

And damn it, regardless of what common sense told him, he still wanted her.

Now maybe more than ever.

Chapter Three

Libby punched her pillow hard, shoved it this way and that, but it didn't help her get comfortable. And she knew why.

For three weeks now, she'd tried to forget the big lug and his compelling dark eyes. Her first foray into sexual matters had been less than awe-inspiring—if she ignored the way he'd made her feel. But she couldn't. She remembered it oh too well. Every single shiver and tremor and spark and gasp. It plagued her mind and left her achy and fidgety and . . . needy. She didn't like it. She didn't like him.

So *why* couldn't she get him out of her head?

Flopping to her back and throwing an arm over her face, Libby tried to block out the memory of how exciting he'd been, how sexy—up until the moment he'd turned into such a jerk.

He'd called her a baby. Now there was a laugh. Maturity was her middle name. Losing her mother so young had forced her to grow up quick, to plan her life long before most kids even thought about tomorrow, much less years down the road. She was mature all right—but given the tantrum she'd had on him, he'd never believe that now.

Of course, she'd never see him again, so what did his beliefs matter?

It mattered, blast him, because he'd gotten her all primed, showed her what she'd been missing, then turned as prim as a maiden aunt. All his suave, macho confidence had melted beneath sputtering incredulity.

All because she was a *little* younger than him.

How old was he anyway? Thirty-three or four? Certainly not old. Twelve years was no biggie. Not to her. Not to most men.

She'd considered asking Uncle Elwood about him, but luckily she'd snuffed out that idea before it had a chance to take root. Her uncle would have a complete conniption fit if he ever found out that she'd been playing hanky-panky in his gardens. He wanted her to study, graduate nursing school, and remove herself from his responsibilities.

And she would, as fast as humanly possible.

This meant she needed to relegate good ole Brown Eyes to the status of an opportunity missed, and stop thinking of him. That should have been easy to do. Never before had she had a problem dismissing guys. First there'd been the grief for her mother. Then the uncertainty of living with Elwood. And her studies. Her determination.

Guys just hadn't factored into her priorities.

Before meeting *him*.

But now he had her so blasted curious, she thought she might implode. In one short, unsuccessful interlude, he'd managed to turn her into a sex maniac. She wanted to find out all there was to the whole intimacy game. Maybe the time had come for her to notice the masculine sex.

Other guys wouldn't mind her age or inexperience. She knew plenty of men, from college, from working, even from the hospital. When she smiled at them, they always smiled back. They seemed delighted by her attention. And a few of them even had dark brown eyes.

Not eyes like his, but . . .

Tough tootsies. Her choices were limited, so she'd have to make do. But first things first. She wasn't a dumb girl to mess up her life because of a little sexual exploration. She was a woman of the new millennium. A modern woman. If she intended to be sexually active—and she sort of did—then there were certain precautions to take.

She'd set an appointment first thing tomorrow. Not with a doctor at the hospital. Heaven forbid her uncle should get wind of her private plans! No, she'd hunt in the phone book, pick someone out of the way, and take care of business.

Then she'd find a guy who suited. There had

to be one out there for her. And maybe looking would prove fun.

Mind made up, Libby punched her pillow one last time and settled in to sleep. But sometime during the night, dark brown eyes and a sensual smile invaded her dreams, and she knew in her heart that any man other than him would simply be a substitute.

Since she didn't even know Brown Eyes's name, a substitute was all she could have.

It'd been damn near a month. A *month* of celibacy and Axel couldn't take it. Since that fantasy-inspired interlude in the garden, he'd been turning women down. It was enough to curdle his blood. He was worse than a married man. At least they had wives at home. All he had was one super sexy young lady who had turned him inside out for reasons he couldn't begin to understand.

Letting her occupy his mind in his off hours was bad enough, but no way in hell would he let her affect his work. When in the office, he had only the well-being of each patient on his mind.

He snatched up a file on his desk, determined to read the medical history on the young lady he'd see next. A moment later, his thoughts back in order, he nodded. His newest patient appeared healthy as a horse. No history of serious medical problems. She only needed a routine exam to get a prescription for birth control.

Wearing his doctor face, Axel went down the

hall to exam room three. Along the way, Nora—
who was both a nurse in his employ and his best
friend's wife—fell into step beside him.

Nora said, "This one is a little skittish. I take it
she's never seen a gynecologist before."

Axel nodded. "Thanks. We'll try to make her
at ease." As he opened the door and drifted in,
Nora on his heels, he was already saying, "Good
afternoon, Ms. Preston. How are you to—"

Her screech of horror made his hair stand on
end.

Axel back-stepped and bumped into Nora,
who bumped into the hallway wall.

"What in the world?" Nora sputtered.

But Axel couldn't say a damn thing. There *she*
was, on his exam table, buck naked except for a
paper sheet. "Good Lord," he rasped, his aplomb
thoroughly shot to hell.

"Get out!" she yelled, and then in utter horror, *"Shut the door."*

His brows came down in a snap. To Nora, Axel
said, "I know her. Give us a moment, please." He
did shut the door—but with him on the inside.

"Kindly lower your voice."

Wide-eyed and white-faced, a pulse wild in
her throat, she stared at him. Her small hands
clutched that paper sheet so tight, he could see
every single curve beneath. Not good.

Turning his back, Axel drew in a calming
breath. "My entire waiting room is probably
agog with curiosity after that scream."

She said, "Ohmigod. Ohmigod, I'm sorry.
Just . . . please. Get out."

Axel peeked at her over his shoulder. It wasn't

easy. In fact, it was damn hard. But he kept his gaze on her face. "There's no reason to be so embarrassed."

Her mouth fell open. "No reason . . . You idiot, I'm *naked*."

Don't go there. Don't go there. He resolutely cleared his mind of all sexual images. He was a doctor, a damn good doctor, a concerned, caring medical professional—who had never been in quite such a predicament.

He hadn't even had a chance to tell her to scoot down.

He swallowed a groan. "I'll step out," he assured her in a rush before she fainted, which she looked ready to do. "You can get dressed, and then we'll talk."

Her mouth dropped open again and just as quickly snapped shut. "We have absolutely *nothing* to say to each other. Nothing. Now *leave.*"

The hell they didn't. She'd come to him to get on the pill, after claiming to be a virgin. Apparently she meant to remedy that awesome circumstance.

He faced her fully, crossed his arms over his requisite white coat, and glanced at her small bare feet. So dumb, but even that little glimpse at pink toes, for crying out loud, and his stomach muscles tightened.

"You came here for birth control. If you don't want me as your doctor—"

"Ha!" As if hunting for something to throw at him, she looked around his office. Holding the sheet tight with one hand, she stretched over to grab a metal tray.

Axel held up a hand. "I can recommend someone."

She froze in midreach. "Are you out of your mind?"

"Uh, no."

She clutched that stupid sheet tighter, and Axel prayed the paper wouldn't tear. He watched, just in case, but no, it didn't.

Her chin lifted. "That's such a generous offer," she sneered with a load of sarcasm, "but no thank you. I don't want your help. I don't need your help." And then she went one further, saying, "And I wouldn't trust one of your friends."

"Oh, that's low." He leaned back on the door. "I am a very good doctor, I'll have you know, and I would never recommend someone who wasn't highly qualified."

"That is just *sooo* kind." More and more sarcasm. "But if you'd simply remove yourself, I'll leave and handle my business entirely on my own."

Axel didn't budge. "You want birth control."

"Oh God." She rocked back and forth a little. *"Go. Away."*

He wanted to stay and hash it out with her. He wanted to grab her and kiss her silly. He wanted . . . but no, he had no choice. He had to do as she asked. It was the only decent, professional thing to do. He grabbed the doorknob. "Get dressed and then come to my office."

"Yeah, sure, whatever."

Face stiff, Axel left the room, and a second later he heard the frantic rustle of paper as she all but leaped off the table. He could picture her dressing with the same frenzy she'd employed when dragging up her pants and closing her shirt after he'd given her a screaming orgasm in the chilly gardens of his host's party.

God. Not a good memory at the moment.

He detoured into his private rest room and closed the door. After splashing his face with cold water and giving her plenty of time to dress, he sauntered out and headed for his office. On the outside, he looked calm and in control. He hoped. Because on the inside, every single fiber of his masculinity stood on high alert.

His office door was open, the room empty.

Damn it. Axel strode to the window and jerked up the blinds just in time to see her jump into a beat-up old Ford Escort and gun the motor. She ground the gears, squealed the tires, and drove away as if wild dogs nipped at her heels.

He dropped the blinds with a clatter, so frustrated he wanted to—

"Would you like to tell me what's going on?"

Taken unaware, Axel spun around to see Nora standing in his doorway. He tried to wipe all expression from his face.

She smiled, closed the door, and leaned on it. "Come on, Axel. What's going on?"

"Nothing."

"Mmm hmmm." Her disbelief was palpable. "I'll just call Cary and see if he knows anything about—"

"No, don't tell him!" Frustration mounting, Axel ran a hand through his hair, then dropped into his leather chair. He had about two minutes before his next patient would expect him.

His attempt at a lighthearted laugh fell flat. "It's really stupid."

"I expected no less of you."

He made a face. Nora had been married to his best friend for three years now. True, she'd seen both sides of him, the respected, serious doctor and the take-it-easy, live-life-to-the-fullest playboy. Never before had the two collided with quite so much fanfare.

Naturally, Nora would enjoy sharing his plight with others. She knew that he'd harassed Cary plenty when Cary fell in love with her, just as he'd done to his brother, Booker, when Booker had gone head over ass in love with Frances. Not that Axel intended to fall in love. Hell no.

He'd only just learned Libby's name!

But this little debacle could count as woman trouble, if either Cary or Booker wanted to stretch the facts. If they learned that a woman— a patient, no less—had screamed at the sight of him, they'd give him crap till the day he died.

"Ahem." Nora tapped her rubber-soled shoe. "I can have Cary on the phone in less than a minute."

Axel gave up with a groan. "She's . . . some-one I met at a party."

"And?"

"We got mildly involved."

"Mildly involved? What does that mean, ex-actly?"

Axel leveled her with a look. "You really don't want details, now do you?"

"Oh." Nora drew back with a frown. "And she wanted you to be her gynecologist? How odd."

He could understand her astonishment. "It's not like that. She didn't know it was me."

Shaking her head, Nora said, "She didn't know what was you?"

Axel shoved to his feet to pace. "We never got to the name exchange, all right? We hit it off—sexually, that is. We just sort of went with it. Then things went wrong—and no, you don't want details about that either. We parted company, end of story."

And since then, he'd thought of her at least every other minute.

"But you never learned her name?"

He tapped the file on his desk. "I know it now. Libby Preston."

Nora slowly shook her head. "Lord, Axel, this is incredible, even for you."

"Yeah, I know." He rubbed his face. "When she screamed, I damn near had a heart attack."

Fighting a grin, Nora said, "I had a heck of a time explaining things to the women in the waiting room."

He could only imagine. "What'd you tell them?"

"That a sonogram had shown triplets."

Axel laughed. "Good thinking. That's enough to make any woman shout." He immediately sobered. "I wanted to talk to her."

"So talk to her."

"I can't." Remembering the way she'd laid rubber in the parking lot, he scowled. "She ran out on me."

"So now you have her name. You even have her phone number and address."

Removing temptation, Axel shoved the file toward Nora. "That'd be unethical in the extreme. Given her reaction here, I'd say she obviously doesn't want to see me."

"No!" Feigning shock, Nora gaped at him. "It can't be. A woman who'd reject you? I'll be disillusioned for life."

"Ha ha." But to set the record straight, Axel explained, "I sort of embarrassed her. By . . . sort of rejecting her first."

"Uh-huh. And?"

"She's only twenty-one."

"So?"

"I'm thirty-five, Nora. A sophisticated doctor. A seasoned womanizer."

Nora rudely laughed.

"I am, damn it." Hands shoved in his pockets, he muttered, "She's barely out of high school."

"I took her history, Axel. She's twenty-one, totally legal by anyone's standards. If you like her—"

"*Like* has nothing to do with it." Lust drove him, nothing more. Pure, unadulterated, unfulfilled lust. "In fact, I'm not sure I do. Like her, that is."

"Of course you don't."

Axel narrowed his eyes on Nora. Since marrying Cary, she'd gotten awfully cheeky. "The young lady has a temper that could flay a man alive. And she doesn't moderate what she says. And she's a . . ."

"A what?"

He pinched his mouth shut. Libby's sexual history, or rather lack of history, was listed on her file, but he wouldn't discuss that with anyone. "Never mind." And then, "Her name is Libby. A pretty name, huh?"

Nora rolled her eyes. "Mrs. Culligan is waiting on you. And if you've never waited naked in a paper sheet on a cold plastic table, then let me tell you, it's excruciating."

Axel knew that. He made it a point to be especially sensitive to the needs of his patients, and he went out of his way to make the ladies feel as comfortable with him as he could. He never kept them waiting, was always as gentle as humanly possible, and treated every woman with extreme respect.

Which meant his personal woes would have to go on the back burner for now. "Right. Let's go."

Nora shoved Libby's file back across his desk with deliberate provocation. "Take care of business. Finish out the day. Then *call her*. If she tells you to lose her number, then yes, calling again would be a breach of professionalism. But until you call, until you give it a shot, you just don't know." And with that instruction, Nora left the room.

Knowing he couldn't make a rational decision right now, Axel followed. And because he really did care about the women he treated, he succeeded in stifling all thoughts of Libby.

At least until his last patient left.

Then he sat down at his desk, picked up her file—and finally made up his mind on what to do.

* * *

At seven o'clock, with the sun still out and birds still singing, Libby curled into the corner of her open hide-a-bed, wearing a nightshirt, a rumpled sheet over her lap, only half watching the kick-ass movie she'd rented from the video store. She didn't want to go to bed yet, but she didn't really want to stay up either. She felt miserable. Cold on the outside, hot on the inside. Achy and mortified and mind-numb with the reality of what had happened.

Her toenails were now painted purple, she'd put intricate braids into her hair, and she'd given herself a facial. None of that had been distraction enough. An uneaten quart of cherry cordial ice cream sat on the end table, a soup spoon spiked into the middle. She'd meant to have a binge, but somehow, that didn't really appeal either.

Moving to Timbuktu appealed. Changing her name and her identity appealed. Raping one very delectable doctor . . . No. She detested him, and the embarrassment he'd caused her. She really, really did. Sort of.

Blast it, she was lonesome. And *soooo* mad.

But it was red-hot, unbearable humiliation that she suffered from most of all.

Groaning aloud, she curled in on herself and for the millionth time relived that awful moment when Dr. Dean had stepped into the exam room. Her heart had shot into her throat and her stomach had bottomed out when those brown eyes she remembered so well had locked with hers—then skipped down her sheet-covered body.

Thank God her feet weren't in the stirrups.

She hadn't been sure about that part, if she was supposed to be ready when he came in or if he'd want to talk first. Luckily she'd decided to remain stiff and straight until instructed to do otherwise.

At first, he'd looked very much the doctor, professional but detached—then scorching recognition had flooded his expression. *After* she screamed.

She curled tighter, half laughing at herself, half moaning in tortured agony. She'd actually done that, screamed like a raving lunatic and ordered him out of his own office. Wearing no more than a sheet. Waiting for him to . . .

No! *No, no, no.* She was not going to keep thinking about it.

So she'd screamed. Big deal. Under the circumstances, screaming seemed a reasonable, perfectly understandable reaction to discovering his true identity.

Oh why oh why did he have to do *that* for a living? And why, out of all the docs in town, did she make an appointment at that one particular office? Once again, fate had dealt her a raw deal. She and fate were now on very bad terms.

There were no answers to the questions she'd already asked herself over and over again. She shoved back the sheet and padded barefoot toward the fridge to put the ice cream away before it melted. Halfway to her kitchenette, a knock sounded on her door. Never mind that it was Friday night. Never mind that she was a single woman at a very dateable age. She never got company, and she didn't want any now. She continued on and shoved the ice cream into the freezer.

But ignoring her unwelcome visitor did no good because the knock came again and again until she stomped across the floor and flung the door open.

A potent, dark brown gaze captured her. "Hello."

She actually stumbled back a step before forging forward again. "You!"

He leaned one shoulder on the doorframe and casually—like she wouldn't notice—stuck his big, booted foot in the doorway so she couldn't slam it on his handsome face.

"Yeah, me." He gave her a quick once-over, frowning at her braids before meeting her gaze with a look of accusation. "You left without saying good-bye."

Libby blinked at him in disbelief. He came to her dinky apartment because he felt slighted? What a buffoon.

What a sexy hunk of a buffoon.

She'd seen him at the party wearing a dress shirt and slacks, and at his office wearing the clichéd white coat and casual tie. Now he wore an ancient T-shirt with a football logo on the front and broken in, faded jeans that looked soft, comfortable, and casual.

No matter what he wore, he looked too delicious for words. "Trust me," she told him, ignoring his inviting appearance, "I was hardly in the mood for friendly conversation."

He looked her over again, slower this time,

lingering in impolite places and making her wish she wore sweats and a thick housecoat. Suddenly he realized he was doing it and snapped his attention back to her face. "May I come in?"

"No. Anything else?"

His long, drawn out sigh fanned her face. "Could I at least apologize?"

Her eyes narrowed. "For what?"

Clearing his throat, he said, "Well, for making you scream." And in a lower, sincere voice, "I'm sorry you were embarrassed. If it's any consolation, I was plenty shocked, too."

No consolation at all. "You weren't naked and on a table."

"No." His mouth twitched. "But I'm a doctor. A professional. Despite our . . . association, I would have—"

Libby drilled his hard chest with her finger. "Not in this lifetime, bud."

A smile brought out golden lights in his dark eyes. "I understand. Again, I apologize. Now please, let me in. I want to talk to you."

"Are you done apologizing?"

Wary, he said, "No?"

"You don't know?"

He huffed. "All right. I'm sorry for calling you a baby, too. Obviously, despite the odd braids in your hair, you're a mature young lady. But you are young and it threw me. I figured you to be much older."

"Ignore the braids. I was bored. But on the inside, where it counts, I'm an old lady."

He didn't look like he believed her. "I haven't been with anyone your age since I was eighteen."

Exasperation exploded from her. "Oh, for heaven's sake. You're saying you're into older women?"

"Experienced women," he clarified. "Because I accept who and what I am—"

"And that is?"

"Not a conversation for your hallway." He stiffened, put out and fed up. "Now let me in."

Libby examined a fingernail. "You were apologizing?" she prompted.

Seconds ticked by while tension thickened in the air. "All right. I'm also sorry that I . . . well . . ."

"Left me hanging?" she offered, her temper flaring again at the awful memory. "Gave me a bite, but not the whole meal? Led me on? Implied false promises? Made—"

He bent and kissed her, hard and fast. "I get the point," he growled, "and yes, I'm sorry for that, too."

Libby went mute. Even that, a smacking kiss that lasted less than a nanosecond, and she was ready to invite him in.

Still leaning far too close to her mouth, he said, "It was a first for me, and it's plagued me ever since."

Libby licked her lips, and because he was close, she tasted his lips, as well. "Plagued you how?"

He stepped in, crowding her back with his big body and closing the door behind him. He smelled good, like aftershave and fresh air and hot male. His wind-rumpled hair made her fingers itch to touch it. His five o'clock shadow made her skin tingle, imagining how it'd feel.

He stared at her, filling her with the swelling warmth she remembered oh so well.

"In every way known to man." He leaned back on the door, his gaze level, probing, saying more than his words could. "I can't stop thinking about you. I can't stop thinking about what might have happened if I hadn't blundered so badly. And most of all, I can't stop thinking about how nice it likely would have been to make love to you."

"Oh." So maybe they were finally on the same track.

His hands closed over her shoulders, slowly dragging her closer. "And on that note . . . I'd like to help if I can."

Chapter Four

Damn, she was sweet, Axel thought, watching the way her thick eyelashes lowered over her blue eyes and her lips parted. Sweet and so damn ready. He'd never tortured himself before. It sucked. But he felt a vested interest in her now. In a way, he'd gotten things started and now he felt compelled to involve himself further. He owed her that much.

The feeling was odd because, other than sexual satisfaction, he'd never really felt he owed a woman before. He stuck with experienced women who knew the score and wanted no more than he offered. He avoided virgins and young hopefuls, and kept a clear conscience because of it.

But not this time.

Libby slowly went on tiptoes, putting her mouth level with his. She clasped her hands around his neck and in a husky, *take me* voice, said, "What do you suggest?"

Oh, he had suggestions, all right.

No. *Get a grip, Axel.*

He caught her elbows and moved her back, putting some necessary space between them. That spontaneous kiss he'd planted on her mulish mouth was unfortunate. Sure, it had shut her up real quick, but it also gave her the wrong idea.

"As I started to say earlier, I know who and what I am."

"So enlighten me."

He intended to. "I'm a man who enjoys his freedom, a man who takes his job seriously, but not much else, including commitment. I would make a lousy significant other and an even worse husband."

"Did I propose and forget about it?"

"No, but women your age—"

Her eyes narrowed, but he didn't let it put him off.

"—they tend to get emotionally involved in physical relationships."

"And naturally, you don't."

"No. Never. If you don't believe me, you could ask my brother, Booker, or my best friend, Cary. They both succumbed to marriage years ago, but I like variety—in women and in everything else."

"Bully for you. So what exactly is it you think to offer me?"

"Advice."

She blinked. "Come again?"

"I'd like to offer you some advice."

Her neck stiffened. Her shoulders went back—which drew his attention to her breasts, barely concealed by a cotton nightshirt with teddy bears decorating it. Christ, *teddy bears*?

"Advice on . . . ?"

Pacing away from her and her girlish—and somehow super sexy—nightwear—Axel finally noticed his surroundings. He stumbled to a halt. A bed. Right *there*, within easy reach. "Uh . . . Why do you have a bed in the middle of the floor?"

"It's where I sleep."

Had she been curled up, warm and cozy, when he knocked? He gulped. He glanced at his watch. "You were already in bed?"

With a shrug in her voice, she said, "Watching a movie." She gave an evil grin. "About a woman who beats up men."

Axel looked around and frowned.

"Yeah, I know, the place is small. The bed folds up to a loveseat, but since I never have company, I don't bother with it very often."

So she always had a bed, right there, in the middle of her floor? He cleared his throat and tried to put that cozy-looking nest of blankets from his mind. Facing Libby, he clasped his hands behind his back and tried to appear impersonal. "You came to me today for birth control. I assume that means you intend to become sexually active."

"Wow. You are *so* perceptive." Arms crossed and head tilted in a challenging way, she said, "So?"

Damn. She didn't even deny it. He struggled for the right words. How in hell did fathers handle this stupid talk? It was harder than he'd ever suspected. "Since, as you claimed, I gave you your first orgasm, I feel responsible."

Red-hot color flooded her face. "Good grief, you're ballsy!"

"I know." He shrugged, not really repentant since it was true. "But you did tell me it was your first—"

"I told you that when I thought things were going to happen between us. Since they're not . . . They're not, right?"

Say no, say no . . . Axel rubbed the back of his neck and spouted his well-rehearsed speech. "Young virgins have a way of assimilating sex with love. Since, like I explained, I'm not in the market for anything serious, I don't want to mislead you."

Disgust washed away her embarrassment. "Yeah, don't mislead the poor dumb virginal child." She turned away, heading for the door as if she thought he'd follow. "Rest assured, my private business is no business of yours. You owe me nothing. But in case you've forgotten, I already told you I wasn't in the market for serious involvement either. I've got my life all planned out and some bozo with overcharged hormones doesn't figure into things, even if he's stupendous in the sack—which you sure as certain haven't proved."

She kept challenging him, and damn it, he kept rising to the challenge, in more ways than one. He hoped like hell she wouldn't notice his Jones pushing against the stiff fabric of his jeans.

She went on, thankfully keeping her narrowed eyes on his face. "Between college and work and an uncle who wants me out of his life, I don't have time for distractions, at least, not a distraction that takes more than a night or two."

She reached the door and put her hand on the doorknob, looking at him expectantly. Axel stared back. Oh no, he wasn't about to leave. Not yet.

"A night or two?" he questioned.

"That's right." She shrugged. "I'm twenty-one. Since Mom died six years ago, I've spent every available minute working toward independence. You might see me as a naïve babe, but let me tell you, doc, there's nothing naïve about a fifteen-year-old girl left homeless."

Fifteen. Damn. Overwhelming sympathy damn near choked him up. He wanted to hold her. He wanted to hug her and console her six years too late. "I am so sorry—"

"Don't you dare." She raised an imperious hand. "The last thing I want from you is pity. I don't need it. My uncle eventually took me in so I had a roof over my head and food to eat."

Eventually? What the hell did that mean? And she mentioned the basics, but had she been given love? Had she gotten all the things a young girl needed from her parents? Axel didn't know, and looking at her set face didn't tell him a damn thing.

Regaining his attention, she said, "But understand something here, doc."

"Call me Axel."

She did a double take. "That's your name?"

He half grinned. "Afraid so."

She ignored that to continue on her tirade. "Right. So anyway, Axel, I worked my tush off and graduated high school when I was seventeen. Thanks to my GPA, I earned several grants and scholarships, but not enough to pay for a four-year program to get my BSN. Because my uncle wanted me to feel financially responsible for good grades, he insisted that I pay half of my remaining college expenses."

"You're working your way through?"

"In a way. I took a year off before starting college and took any job I could find. Other than what I paid my uncle for room and board—"

"He charged you?" No way could Axel hide his incredulity. What type of abnormal relative was he anyway?

She rolled her shoulder. "Sure he did. I was still living with him then. But other than what I had to give him, I saved every dime until I made enough to get started. Working part-time has slowed me down a bit, so I have one more year of nursing school before I graduate. But don't think for a single second that I'm going to let you or anyone else get in my way."

She sounded equally proud of herself and defiant. And full of spirit. Axel stared at her in wonder, and burgeoning respect. "I had no idea."

"Yeah, well, you never bothered to ask. But somehow that doesn't surprise me. You seem like the thick-headed sort to run wild with assumptions, especially where women are concerned."

She dished out more insults than any female he'd ever known. It wasn't what he was used to. Ready to get some of his own back, he said, "I realize name-calling is a sure sign of adolescence, but do you think we could stick to the point?"

Temper snapped her spine straight and brought her storming away from the door and back to him. She appeared so livid that Axel braced himself, thinking she might slug him. Instead she went nose to nose with him and snarled, "The point is that I might be young, doc, but I prefer that to being old and set in my ways."

"Damn it, call me Axel." He scowled. "And I am not *old*."

"Forty is old."

"Forty! But I'm only—" He caught sight of the satisfaction twinkling in her eyes and knew she'd just gigged him on purpose. "Brat." And to make sure she knew, he added, "I'm thirty-five as of a few months ago."

"Downright ancient." She snickered. "You old people are so easy to provoke."

In soft warning, Axel said, "You're just begging for it, aren't you?"

"No way, buster." She crossed her arms under her breasts again. "Not anymore. A few weeks ago, sure, you had me to the begging point. But in case you've forgotten, you went off in a huff and I didn't hear from you—"

"I had no idea how to reach you."

Blue eyes fried him. "Like you would have?"

No way would he admit to anything with her so antagonistic.

She sniffed. "That's what I thought. Not that

it matters because now I've got my sights set on *younger* game."

That bugged him worse than anything else she'd said. "Who?"

"I don't know yet." She went to her bed and flopped down onto the corner, curling her bare legs beneath her. "But it can't be that hard to find an agreeable guy, right?" With a coy look, she added, "Someone young and open to new experiences, like virginity."

Feeling protective again—and, damn it, jealous—Axel circled the bed and seated himself on the edge of the mattress beside her. "Your virginity is something special, Libby. Don't throw it away."

"Yeah, it's so special it left you speechless and running off like a scared rabbit."

"I was *not* scared. Have you been listening to anything I've said?"

"Whatever. Holding onto my virginity has lost its appeal." She patted his chest. "Thanks to you and that little taste in the garden, I'm just dying to find out what I've been missing."

Axel's guts cramped with the urge to show her. He covered her hand on his chest to keep it still. "Don't go out with anyone you don't know well."

"Thanks, gramps. But I'm not stupid. I'm not looking to get strangled."

Tamping down his annoyance at her continued jabs at his age, Axel gripped her wrist and urged her closer toward him. "I'm glad to hear it. But don't think birth control pills will cover all the bases. These days you need a—"

"Condom. Rubber. Raincoat. Yeah, I know. STDs and all that." She wrinkled her nose. "It almost makes sex unappealing, huh?"

To his mind, nothing could make sex with her unappealing.

"I guess that's one reason I didn't rush into bed with anyone." She looked at his mouth, and her voice softened a bit. "I have been busy, and the idea of having to get a clean bill of health from any interested males just seems very unromantic."

He could show her appealing. He could show her romantic. Instead he thought of a few questions he wanted to ask. "You don't live with your uncle anymore?"

Her gaze came back to his. "Like I said, he kept me housed and fed when I was underage. But he never had children of his own because he didn't want them—then he got saddled with me. Believe me, he's made no bones about the inconvenience of raising his sister's kid." She lifted a hand and swept it around her. "Hence my apartment. He said he'd prefer to pay rent than have me underfoot, and he figures I'll learn to take care of myself this way. Like I didn't already know how to do that. Believe me, between Mom's crazy lifestyle and my uncle's disinterest, I've been taking care of myself for a long time."

"So your uncle pays the rent for this place?"

She nodded. "Yeah, but I've kept a tally of everything he's spent, and I intend to pay him back as soon as possible."

Scowling, Axel looked around at the miniscule efficiency apartment. It wasn't very close to the local college and it couldn't be all that safe, considering the neighborhood.

He decided her uncle must be a real prick.

"That's why you were working at the party the other night?"

"I still take any odd job that doesn't interfere with my class schedule so I can make headway in paying him back."

Somehow, Axel's free hand had gotten into her braids and he cradled her skull. And even worse, she leaned toward him, her head slightly tipped back, her mouth *that* close.

An admission was torn from him. "Damn it, but I hate the idea of you experimenting with some yahoo who may or may not show you the right way of things."

Taunting, egging him on, she eased closer still. "I don't have much choice . . . now do I?"

He could give her choices. He could give her mind-numbing pleasure . . .

Her small pink tongue came out to lick at her lips. "So . . . you said you'd thought about it, about me?"

Every day, damn near every minute. Not that he'd confess such a thing to her. "It was a memorable event."

She put her other hand on his chest—right over his now thundering heart. "I have too," she admitted. "The last few days, I haven't been able to eat. I haven't even been able to sleep. I've barely been able to study."

Regrettably, he said the first thing that came to his mind. "You're too thin to be skipping meals."

Her provocative expression gave way to blank surprise, then she rolled her eyes and half laughed. "Too thin, huh? Are you sure you're good at this seduction stuff? Because from what I've seen, you're batting a big fat zero."

Axel locked his jaw, feeling guiltier by the second. He didn't want to put her in a funk and have her skipping meals on his account—not if he could relieve her. And he sure as hell didn't want to distract her from her studies, not when they were so important to her. "I'm good," he assured her. "And you should already know from our first encounter, thin or not, I have no complaints with your body."

Her fingers curled, stroking his chest, testing his pecs with sensual curiosity. "Same here." She looked down at his mouth again. "Never in my life did I do anything as crazy as I did at that party. I'm usually the most level-headed, circumspect gal around. But that night . . . everything just felt right."

And that described the problem in a nutshell. He wasn't the type of guy that she should feel *right* with.

Axel half turned away, and her hands knotted in his T-shirt, bringing him back around. "For a fling, doc. For an experiment. Not right as in life-altering or earth-shattering or till death do us part." She tried to shake him, smiling, exasperated. "Just . . . right for that moment. Between us."

Axel closed his eyes. "I am not an honorable man, Libby."

"Is that so?"

He drew a breath, and met her gaze. "Outside of my work, which always comes first, I'm a selfish bastard and I know it. Hell, everyone knows it. But even so, I don't want to hurt you."

Libby bit her lip, fighting a laugh. "But don't you see? I don't really give a flip if you're selfish. Be any kind of obnoxious, egotistical chump that you want, it won't matter to me, because other than sexually, I have no interest in you at all." Her nose touched his. "Now, if you're saying you're selfish in bed, then—"

"No." He gave up. Hell, to be honest, he'd given up the moment he saw her in his office and knew he'd be able to find her again. "You'll enjoy yourself, I guarantee it."

Her breath snagged on a sigh, her eyes turned hopeful. "Does that mean . . . ?"

"Yeah." He looked at her crazy braids, her teddy bear shirt, and her purple toenails, and was gripped by the most violent lust he'd ever experienced. He was already hard. His hands were shaking. His stomach knotted.

But he knew it wasn't *just* lust. Lust was a familiar thing, and this was . . . more. Hotter, gentler, explosive and tender. Consuming.

It left him floundering. Lust he understood. The other stuff . . . Too unfamiliar to examine closely. "I want you, Libby. Right now. Right here." He touched her cheek, and was struck by the incredible warmth of her velvety skin. "You okay with that?"

She came up to her knees and her eyes darkened—with uncertainty or excitement? "Yeah, I am."

Axel eyed the short, narrow bed. It didn't look big enough to accommodate two people, but he'd make do. At the moment, he could take her standing up. Hell, he could take her standing on his head.

He just really, really needed to take her.

They stared at each other, Libby waiting for him to make a move, Axel trying to determine what the best move might be for a virgin.

Getting her naked topped his list, so he asked, "Have you seen any nude men?"

Her eyes widened. "Not yet, but don't let that stop you."

His grin came reluctantly. She was a cheeky little thing, quick with a comeback, a delightful mix of shyness and bravado.

Having no modesty to speak of, Axel reached back, grabbed a fistful of his T and yanked it off over his head. Watching her watch him, he dropped it to the floor and simply stood there. He liked the way she stared at his chest and abdomen, sort of agog, her eyes rounded and her lips slightly parted. Her gaze dipped lower still, visually tracing the bulge in his jeans.

When he didn't move, she said, "Go on."

Axel laughed as he pulled off his boots, then sat on the side of the mattress to peel off his socks. Leaving his jeans on for the moment, he settled back into the corner where she'd been earlier. The back of the love seat served as a headboard of sorts, but with arms. Axel caught her waist and pulled her onto his lap.

She might be tall, but she didn't weigh much, and she was soft in all the right places.

"The braids are cute," he told her, "but how hard would it be to lose them?"

Both her hands were on him, stroking through his chest hair with single-minded absorption. "Not hard."

"Great." He lifted one skinny braid and the cloth-covered band holding it slid off the end. Her hair was so thick and silky, the braid unraveled with no help from him. In minutes, he had all eight braids undone. Her hair looked slightly wavy now, but after stroking his fingers through it, it smoothed out. "I love your hair," he told her, his voice going a little deep with the reality of having her so close, his for the night.

He just had to keep his cool and make it good for her. From what he remembered—how many years ago was it?—virgins were tricky. They needed more care. More time. More finesse.

He could handle it. Maybe. If he thought about other things, like getting the oil changed in his BMW, or facing the chief of staff over a reprimand, or how Booker and Cary would react if they knew the predicament he currently faced.

"Will you kiss me again?"

"Damn right." Axel took her mouth, slow and deep and wet, his fingers tangled in her hair, her fingers on his shoulders, kneading like a cat. She squirmed on his lap, distracting him with the way her bottom moved against his boner. And thinking of her bottom . . . His hands went there without his mind's permission, and damn, she felt good.

The television played in the background, but

not loud enough to cover the sounds of their deepened breathing.

Forgetting his own rules about slow and careful, Axel turned and laid her flat beneath him across the bed. One of her slender legs got trapped between his, the other rested alongside his hip. She made a soft sound of surprise, hugging him tighter to her, arching up, provoking him.

"Shhh," he whispered, raising his head to look at her. Her eyes were heavy, her mouth swollen and deep pink from their kisses. "Be still, Libby. Relax."

"No." She pushed up again, her hands spread wide across his lower back. Her eyes closed in pleasure. "You feel *so* good. All hard thick muscle. I like being squashed."

He didn't want to squash her, damn it. "Libby . . ."

"Do you ever think about this with your female patients?"

Appalled, Axel thrust himself away on stiffened arms. "Good God, no!"

"Really?" With him above her, she explored his chest again, dragging her palms over his nipples, sliding one hand down to his abdomen, making him nuts. "I heard that gynecologists see women the same way a mechanic sees a car engine. Is that true then?"

"I really don't want to talk about my work right now." Talking about it gave him the willies, and made him very uncomfortable. The women he saw as patients . . . No, he never thought of them in sexual terms.

Thank God Libby hadn't been a patient.

Her hands opened on his jeans-covered ass, slid into his back pockets, and squeezed. "The thing is," she whispered, suddenly looking shy, "I didn't feel funny about you seeing me naked until I found out what you do."

Oh. Axel relaxed, realizing the source of her questions. He came down to his elbows and pressed a tender kiss to her mouth. She sighed and her warmth drew him again, so he continued kissing her, lingering a little more each time, licking over her lips, then sinking in for a long, leisurely, tongue-twining smooch that left her breathless and grasping at him.

"What I do at the office," he said while working his way from her lips to her ear then her throat, "has nothing to do with this. I separate my work from any sort of intimacy."

"But . . ."

"No buts, honey. I can't say I see women as engines. I care too much about their well-being to see them as anything other than living, breathing human beings. But I see them with an eye for health, not beauty. There's nothing sexual in that—and everything sexual in *this*." His hand cupped her breast, gently molding, lifting.

Her lashes sank down, hiding her eyes. She gave a small purr of pleasure and pressed into his palm.

Her breasts were firm and soft, her nipples already painfully tight. He wanted to see her. He wanted to suck on her and hear her moan and see her writhing in excitement.

Axel moved to the side of her, ran his hand

down to her waist, and traced a teddy bear with his fingertip. "Let's get rid of this, okay?"

She bit her lip, then nodded. "You swear you won't be thinking anything medical?"

"I promise it'll be the furthest thing from my mind." He put his hand on her thigh and slowly dragged the thin cotton nightshirt up, up, up, until he could see her sheer panties and her dark pubic hair beneath. His control slipped.

Pausing, he bent, kissed her flat belly, a hipbone, then pressed his mouth to those glossy dark curls.

Libby drew in a deep, broken breath.

In no hurry, Axel inhaled the spicy scent of her—and growled in response. He couldn't wait to taste all of her, to hear her scream again with a climax, and most of all, to sink into her tight and hot and his alone.

A dangerous thought—but undeniable all the same. She would be his, at least for now. And damn it, he liked that idea.

He liked it a lot.

Chapter Five

Libby did her best to hold still as Axel pushed her nightshirt up the rest of the way, dragging his palm over her breast, across her stiffened nipple, until he cupped her shoulder. No matter where he touched, she felt it in other places. Low in her stomach. Between her legs.

A sweet, swirling ache filled her and she wanted to tell him to get on with it, even as she enjoyed his casual lack of haste.

He urged her upright enough that he could remove the sleepwear completely. After tossing it off the other side of the bed, he allowed her to lie back again.

Excited, anxious, and a little uncertain, Libby watched his face to see his reaction to her nudity. He'd said she was thin, but she knew she wasn't skinny. He'd probably seen hundreds, maybe thousands of naked women. Between his sexual freedom and his vocation, naked women were nothing new to him.

Would she measure up?

Given the hot expression in his narrowed eyes, both intense and scrutinizing, he liked what he saw. His mouth tightened, his nostrils flared . . . Libby took a deep breath. He looked so sexy, she could barely wait.

Without diverting his attention from her body, he reached for the snap on his jeans, saying, "Damn, woman, you are irresistible."

Relieved, she gave herself over to the experience of watching a man, in her bed, shuck off his jeans. And Dr. Axel Dean wasn't just any man. Thick with muscle, oozing cocky confidence and blatant sexuality, he was more man than she'd ever met or ever thought to meet.

He eased his zipper down over a rather impressive erection, and in rapid order the jeans came off, along with a pair of snug black boxers. He retrieved his wallet from the back pocket, dug out a condom that he put close at hand, then turned back to her.

Libby got her first up close and personal look at an erect penis.

Truthfully, the whole package was ultra nice. He was firm everywhere, muscular in all the right places, with just enough dark body hair to enhance all his masculinity.

The silky line of hair below his navel to his erection especially intrigued her. It added nice decoration to a rigid abdomen and led the way to that long, solid penis.

"Staring is rude," he told her, smiling a little, balancing himself on his elbow beside her. Biceps flexed with his pose and his heavy, hairy thigh brushed hers, tickling a little. His large dark hand came to rest on her white belly, his fingers idly stroking, as if enthralled with the texture of her skin.

"Is it?" What would an experienced woman say to that? Should she apologize?

"Mmm. But I can maybe hold off for another ten seconds, before I lose it, so for those ten seconds feel free to look all you want."

"What about touching?" She reached out, but he caught her wrist.

"Could be disastrous. Maybe later. After I've had you. Twice."

Still holding her hand, he pressed it up beside her head while moving over her. "You are so warm," he said, nuzzling her neck at a very sensitive spot, teasing her ear, leaving small damp places on her flesh before taking her mouth with voracious hunger.

Kissing she'd done, but not kissing like this. He had a way of making it seem so suggestive, so sensual. So intimate and hot and thrilling. She could kiss him for hours and not tire of it.

His hands came back to her breasts and she tried to gasp, only his mouth was over hers, taking the sound and filling her with his own responding rumble of pleasure. He caught her nipples, rubbing softly with his thumb, then plucking not so softly until she didn't think she could take it anymore. But again, her cries got muffled into low groans.

His hard thigh pressed between hers, and she found herself lifting into him, moving with his body, until it almost seemed they had their own rhythm.

"That's it," he murmured hotly. And rather than come back to her mouth, he kissed his way down her throat to her chest. While cuddling one breast, he closed his mouth over the other, suckling her nipple gently, his rough tongue rasping over her, his teeth nipping.

A very high-pitched, girly sound of excitement filled the air, and Libby realized she had made that sound. But she couldn't help it. Sensation spread through her in pulsing, sizzling waves. Eyes closed, she pressed her head back, feeling those now familiar, explosive tremors swelling and swelling . . .

Axel made a rough sound of approval and continued to suck and tongue and tease her breast. He moved one hand behind the small of her back, then down to her behind, lifting her up so the pressure against her sex became more acute, his whole body stroking, igniting her—and she came.

"Oh God."

His fingers clenched into her bottom, keeping her poised against him, prolonging the orgasm until the very last quiver had left her.

Panting brokenly, her muscles useless, Libby stared at the ceiling and wondered if she was easy or he was just that good.

Struggling to regain her breath, she waited, expecting him to come up to her, maybe hold her, smile at her again.

Instead, she felt his hot, open mouth on her abdomen, his hand now over her behind inside her panties, pushing them down.

She didn't get time to recoup? "Axel . . ." she groaned.

"Say my name again." His tongue dipped into her belly button, then trailed down to the top of her panties. Feeling his mouth there, lightly sucking her skin, tasting her, sent a new rush of sensations crashing over her.

"Oh, uh . . ." Surely he didn't really expect her to be coherent while he did that?

He skimmed her panties down to her knees and she found herself completely naked in front of him. He loomed over her, his palms gliding from her knees up to her thighs and back down again while he stared at her, his expression nearly violent with need, color high on his cheekbones.

Libby held her breath, uncertain, anxious— and suddenly, his fingers dug into her flesh and he pressed her knees apart.

She should have been embarrassed, but the rough, hungry sound he made obliterated rational thought. His fingers moved over her, petting, delving, opening her, and then his mouth was on her *there*, and all she could do was melt.

He slipped off the side of the bed to his knees, moved between her thighs, and pressed them farther apart still, pushing her knees up and back. Oh wow.

His whiskered jaw rasped her inner thigh as he whispered, "You're wet, Libby, and so damn hot." His thumbs opened her, stroked, going deeper and deeper, and then he tasted her, licked, shifted so he could lift her up, giving himself better access, and through it all she panted and twisted and felt another orgasm surging through her tired body.

It was the most unbearable pleasure imaginable. Her hands gripped the sheets hard, as if to anchor herself. So many sensations bombarded her senses—the stroke of his tongue, over her and in her, his hot breath, the sexy sounds of desire he made, the scratch of his beard on places no other person had seen, much less touched.

"Come for me again, baby," he ordered, his tone harsh with demand, and she did, her thighs tightening, her muscles rippling, everything inside her clasping and undulating.

This time he didn't wait. Her mind still spun with disbelief when she heard the tear of foil, felt Axel fumbling near her, then he moved over her, lifted her knees, and pressed inside her.

With little aftershocks still sparking, Libby felt the broad head of his penis pushing past her virginal opening. He stretched her, but in a good way, and given that she'd had two mind-blowing orgasms, she knew it'd be easier for her to accommodate him.

His mouth was wet from her, rubbing against her jawline as he murmured encouragement and hot phrases of need and pleasure. "So tight," she heard him say, and then, darker and with more feeling, "Fuck, yeah."

He sank deeper, his hands holding her face, turning her toward him for a ravenous, eating kiss, and then he was buried inside her, filling her up. Libby held herself perfectly still, panting, trying to get accustomed to the wonderful, taut feeling, the incredible closeness, the emotional intensity that she hadn't expected but relished all the same.

Tears stung her eyes, because she realized he was right. This was more than mere sex. He was the only man who had ever caught and held her attention, the only man to ever distract her from her goals. She didn't know him well, but something about him called to her, brought out emotions she hadn't known she possessed.

By small degrees she got her limbs to move, twining her arms tight around his broad back, lifting her legs to keep him close, and closer still. The new position tilted her pelvis and sent him deeper. She responded with a catch in her breath, freeing her mouth and inadvertently tightening around his thick erection.

Axel held her face and watched her, keeping her gaze captive as he eased out, then thrust, slow, deep, taking it easy, heat pouring off him and off her, their bodies melded together. It was almost too much, that visual connection combined with the pleasure of having him buried inside her. Libby kissed him, biting at his mouth, sucking at his tongue, and with a growl, Axel lost it. He pumped into her, picking up the pace, going faster and harder until suddenly he stiffened, his head back, his teeth locked. He growled, a feral, dark sound of primal satisfaction, his big body shuddering over hers, muscles tight and delineated.

It was the most wonderful, intimate thing Libby had ever experienced. He looked almost dangerous, and then, for a single moment, vulnerable. As his groans faded, his body relaxed and his muscles unclenched. Libby stroked his sweaty shoulders, speechless, awed. His head dropped forward, his dark hair over his brow, his eyes closed. He still labored for breath, but kept his chest off her with stiffened arms.

Feeling a little silly after all that intensity, Libby whispered, "Wow."

His broken laugh turned into a groan, and he went to his back beside her. The moment he left her, she missed him. Her skin now felt cool, her body empty.

One arm covered his eyes but the other held her thigh with blatant possession. Seconds ticked by, measured by the slow beat of her heart, then he lifted his arm and looked at her, his eyes dark and full of triumph.

"You're too far away," he rasped. "Come here." And she did, turning into his side, his arm going around her, keeping her near to him.

Libby had no idea what to do, but she had no complaints with cuddling. After several minutes had passed, he heaved a great sigh and tucked in his chin to look down at her. She met his dark gaze with uncertainty.

Would he leave now? Was he finished with her?

He looked ultimately relaxed and lazy. "You hungry?"

"Ummm . . ." She hadn't expected that. "No, but I can fix you something."

"Stay put. I'll help myself." He patted her hip,

stood, stretched in front of her. "You got a waste can in the bathroom?"

Speechless at his casual attitude, Libby nodded. She watched Axel remove the condom as he headed to her john. His muscled behind was a thing of beauty, especially in motion.

He left the door open, which amazed her, considering a minute later, she heard him flush, then heard him splashing water.

He came out with his face and hair slightly wet, still gloriously naked, and went into her miniscule kitchen. "What movie did you say you rented?" he asked, while rummaging in her fridge.

Well, she didn't have his indifferent attitude toward nudity. She pulled the rumpled sheet up to cover her body and scooted up in the bed, sitting with her legs bent, her arms on her knees. As if the entire day hadn't happened, as if he weren't totally nude, they chatted about food, about the movie, and even about the size of her apartment.

Ten minutes later, Libby found herself snuggled in the dark next to a naked Axel while he fed himself a cheese sandwich with one hand and absently fondled her with the other. The movie she'd missed earlier again played on DVD.

She paid no more attention to it this time than she had the first.

She hadn't expected this careless camaraderie, but it was . . . nice. More than nice.

Halfway through the flick, Axel hugged her a

little and said, "It's getting late," as if the time were no more than an afterthought.

She'd been in a haze of comfort, enjoying his closeness, half asleep, more than a little lethargic. "Is that a hint that you need to go?" Pride forced the words from her constricting throat. "Because I already told you, I'm not going to cause a scene."

"No." He squeezed her closer still so he could kiss her nose. "It's a hint that I'd like to stay the night, maybe make love to you a few dozen times more before the sun comes up. What do you think?" He took the last bite of his sandwich, chewed and swallowed. "Does a sleepover fit in with your independent plans, or should I get my tired, still horny butt out of here and head home to my lonesome bed?"

Stay, her heart screamed, but she pretended to think about it. She really was wiped out, and still achy, and her stomach wasn't all that settled.

Sex, she found, took a lot out of a person. "Can I nap for a while before we indulge in more extracurricular activity?"

"If you don't mind me wrapped around you."

She wouldn't mind that at all. "All right." His natural body warmth felt good, but it wasn't enough. She dragged the blankets a little higher and got comfortable beside him. "You can finish the movie. I'll just doze off."

"Do you need to be somewhere early tomorrow?"

"No, my uncle is expecting me in the afternoon." She made a face. "I'm to serve at another meeting, this one for high tea."

"Pompous ass." Axel shifted in the bed and let her use his chest for a pillow. Aiming the remote, he turned the television volume low. "I'm free for the weekend, so we'll work around your plans."

Did that mean he intended to spend the whole weekend with her? Having sex and doing . . . this? Cuddling and chatting and just being together?

"You sleep," he told her. "I'm going to finish the movie, but I'll wake you up if anything exciting happens."

"Exciting, like . . . ?"

"Like this." He cupped her breast, put several damp, skin-tingling kisses on her neck, and then pulled back with a smile. He smoothed her hair, pressed one last kiss to her forehead, and gave his attention back to the television.

He was the oddest, boldest—and the most wonderful—man she'd ever met. Libby chuckled and, giving into her fatigue, dozed off.

She slept like the dead, like having a man in bed with her was no big deal. On the one hand, Axel supposed he might have worn her out with her first full-fledged sexually satisfying experience. That wasn't an entirely repugnant thought.

On the other hand, he wanted her awake and as turned on as he was.

Since it was well past midnight, he'd let her nap for a few hours. She was curled against him, hot as a Bunsen burner, making him sweat. Time to have more fun.

He slid his arm out from under her so that she lay flat in the bed. Utterly limp, she didn't so much as flicker an eyelash. For a few moments he just looked at her, at her thick dark lashes, her small nose and stubborn chin, and that super sexy, glossy black hair all tumbled.

Normally her skin was very fair, but at the moment, a deep rose chafed her cheeks. Using only his fingertips, Axel smoothed the hair off her forehead and spread it out around her.

She wasn't beautiful, but something about her drew him in and turned him on and made him want to touch her in a hundred different ways—not all of them sexual.

Pushing the sheet down to her knees, then kicking it the rest of the way off her legs, he looked at her nude body. In total relaxation, she appeared very young indeed. Innocent and fresh. Sweet. And undeniably sexy.

Her belly was so pale and soft, her dark, glossy pubic curls a striking and sensual contrast.

Her nipples were now smooth, a deep pink, and very appealing. Unwilling to wait, Axel leaned forward and drew her right nipple into his mouth, sucking gently.

She moaned, her legs shifting a bit, and Axel rested a hand on her flat belly. Another moan, but it didn't sound carnal at all. More like . . . discomfort.

He frowned, lifting his head in alarm. "Libby?" She didn't stir. "Come on, baby, wake up."

She mumbled something in her sleep and turned her head away from him.

A niggling fear skittered through him and Axel put his palm to her forehead.

Scorching heat.

"Shit." Sitting up, he caught her shoulders and gently shook her. "Libby?"

Her eyebrows twitched, her lashes fluttered then opened. Her eyes were bloodshot, unfocused. Her lips looked dry. In a froggy voice, she rasped, "I don't feel good. You should go." And she tried to turn away from him.

Well, hell. "You have a fever, honey. Where's your thermometer?"

She gazed at him in confusion, her eyes vague, her chest laboring painfully. "My what?" She started to shiver and groped blindly for the blankets.

Unbelievable. Axel helped her, pulling the sheet and single blanket back up for her. "I need to take your temperature, sweetheart. You're sick."

Damn it, he should have realized it earlier. She'd felt warm, too warm, each time he'd touched her. Idiot.

He'd thought she was hot for him.

Axel silently cursed himself and pushed out of the bed.

Rather than reply to him, Libby curled onto her side and snuggled tight into the blankets. "Oh God, Axel, I'm freezing."

"I know, baby." 101 problems crowded into his brain. "Do you have anything for fever?"

In strained accusation, her teeth chattering, she groaned, "I never get sick."

"Well, you're sick now." He stalked into her bathroom and looked in the medicine cabinet. It overflowed with female junk, but nothing that would help her. "Where the hell do you keep your medicine?"

When she didn't answer, he went back to her. She looked to be asleep again, but shivers racked her slender body, the blankets up around her ears, her knees curled up to her chest in the fetal position. Sitting beside her, Axel again touched her forehead, then flinched. "Does anything else hurt?"

She frowned, still without opening her eyes. "My chest, a little. I had a stupid cold, but . . ."

Afraid that her cold had developed into pneumonia, Axel pulled her upright and into his arms, cradling her close to his heart. "Listen to me, Libby. I think I should take you to the hospital."

"Oh no." She sounded raw. And very upset at the idea.

Axel cupped her burning cheek. Jesus, she was hot. And she'd said she'd had trouble eating, sleeping. "Listen to me, young lady—"

She pressed against him, trying to lie back down, trying to pull the blankets closer around herself. "Just go away, doc. I'm not your problem, not your patient."

"Don't get stubborn on me now." He held her shoulders, refusing to let her pull away. "You're sick, and from what I can tell, you have nothing here in the way of medicine. You're burning up, but it's too late to call your family physician."

Looking very small and vulnerable, she whispered, "You can't take me to the hospital, Axel."

"Of course I can. They know me there. They'll give you first-rate treatment, I promise."

Eyes closing, she swallowed painfully. "If you do, Uncle Elwood will find out about you."

Elwood.

A rush of blood pounded into Axel's ears. Alarms went off in his head. His throat damn near closed up on him. "Elwood . . . ?"

"Peterson." She peeked up at him, small, frail, the epitome of misery. "He's . . . my uncle."

Oh. Dear. God. Barely squeezing the words out between his clenched teeth, Axel barked, "Your uncle is the *chief of staff*?"

She flinched. "Yes."

Young, a virgin, and now this. Three strikes, and he was out.

Numb, Axel pushed to his feet and stood looking down at her. He couldn't be that unlucky. But to be sure . . . "You're a twenty-one-year-old virgin—whose uncle just happens to be the chief of staff?"

She looked away. "Yes."

"Un-fucking-believable."

Libby jumped at the fury in his tone, took in his appalled expression, and moaned. "Here we go again."

Chapter Six

Never in her life had she felt more miserable. She hurt everywhere, in every bone and joint, and it felt like an elephant sat on her chest. It took enormous effort just to move, just to breathe. But she forced herself into a mostly sitting position and even managed a half-baked smile. Shivering, her teeth clattering together and tears stinging her eyes, Libby rasped, "It's been swell, doc, but I can see the party's over."

Instead of being relieved that she'd let him off the hook, fury darkened his face. "Don't push me, Libby."

Why was he mad? And at the moment, did she even care? She was so damn cold, deep down inside herself, that she couldn't stop shaking. "I know how to treat illness. Remember, I'm a nursing student, soon to graduate. Go with a clear conscience. I'll be fine."

Axel closed his eyes, looked to be counting to ten, then opened them again. Composed, he said, "I'm not leaving you, so forget that."

"You already told me what a self-centered ass you are, remember? It's all right to leave."

"I said no."

She couldn't stay upright a second more. Collapsing back on the bed, freezing, she said, "Bastard."

"Hush." He moved with sudden purpose. "I know what I'll do. I'll call Cary. He'll come over and take care of you."

The very idea of imposing on someone else left her speechless. Why couldn't he just leave her in peace?

Knowing she had to move whether she wanted to or not, she hugged the blankets and started to slide her legs off the side of the bed.

Her feet never touched the floor. In one swoop, Axel pulled her into his arms and held her like a child. That stung. As if her weight were negligible, he strode to the other side of the bed and snagged his jeans.

"Why are you doing this?" He was so wonderfully warm and comfortable that she wanted to crawl inside him. Exhaustion pulled at her, and she laid her head on his hard shoulder.

"You just be quiet." He sat on the side of the bed, holding her, rocking her a little, and used his thumb to press one number on his cell phone.

A second later, some unfortunate soul actually answered.

Axel wasted no time. "Damn Cary, I'm sorry to bug you —what? No, I'm okay. It's Libby. She's . . . If you'll shut up, I'll tell you who she is. She's . . . a woman I'm seeing."

Libby hid her face in his neck. God, this only got worse and worse.

"Damn it, I know you don't know her. But I'm with her now and her uncle is the damn chief of staff . . . Yeah, *Elwood.*" Axel paused, rolled his eyes. "No, I'm not crazy, but for the record I didn't know her uncle was chief of staff. Cary, do *not* laugh, damn you."

Libby realized by the way Axel said Elwood's name that he didn't exactly like him. At least she wasn't alone in that.

"She's sick, maybe pneumonia given her temperature and how fast it came on her. No, she doesn't want to go to the hospital but she's burning up and . . . Yeah, could you? Thanks." He gave her address to his friend, said, "I owe ya," and hung up.

Pressing a kiss to her forehead, he said, "Cary'll be right over. He's a fine doctor, a family practitioner, and he'll know what to do."

"You're a doctor, too," Libby reminded him.

"Wrong kind." He stood again, carrying her as if she weighed no more than a pillow. He entered her tiny bathroom, got a towel off the rack, and using only one hand, doused it in tepid water. "I'm going to wipe you down to try to get your fever under control before Cary gets here."

"No." Libby gripped him with all her puny strength. Logically, she knew it was the fever making her cold, but the idea of anything wet touching her body made her shake that much more.

"Sorry," he said, and went back to the bed where he laid her down, unwrapped her against her protestations, and used the corner of the towel to bathe her face, throat, chest, and arms.

"Oh God." Again, the stupid tears stung her eyes, and she hated herself for it, which made her hate him.

Axel looked as agonized as she felt. "I'm sorry, honey." He kissed her forehead, and continued pressing that cool cloth to her burning body. After a few minutes, it did help, but not enough.

Teeth chattering, Libby said, "I didn't think doctors made house calls anymore."

"Like I said, Cary's a friend."

Axel covered her again, then got dressed and went to put on coffee. Feeling a little more comfortable, Libby half dozed.

A few minutes later, Axel bent near her ear. "I'll be right back."

She stirred enough to ask, "Where are you going?"

"I brought your paperwork with me from my office. Cary might like to see it. Don't move."

No, she wouldn't move. She heard the front door open, and when Axel returned he had someone with him. Libby pulled the covers up over her head. Good grief, she was naked, and couldn't do a thing about it.

"That lump on the bed is her," she heard Axel say. "Libby, Dr. Rupert. Cary, meet Libby Preston."

The bed dipped, and a second later the blanket was pulled from her face. She stared up at a man with rumpled brown hair and tired green eyes and a gentle, kind smile.

"Hello," he said. "I'm Dr. Rupert." Then he stuck a thermometer in her ear, waited all of two seconds and said, "102."

Behind him, Axel fretted. "Pneumonia?"

"Can I tell that from her ear, Axel? No, I can't. Why don't you go sit down somewhere and stop pacing behind me?"

Libby felt just put out enough to say, "Old people tend to fret."

Dr. Rupert's mouth twitched, but he didn't say anything.

Axel wasn't quite so restrained. In low warning, he said, "I'll get even with you for that crack, little girl—but not until you're in full fighting form again."

Libby glared at Axel and clutched the sheet when Dr. Rupert tried to lower it. Utilizing great bedside manner, he said, "Miss Preston, Axel tells me you're to be a nurse, so I'm sure you already know this, but I need to listen to your lungs."

She glared at Axel again. "Turn around."

His eyes widened. "For the love of . . . I've already seen you naked, Libby."

She wanted to kill him. "Not. Like. This."

He threw up his hands. "Fine." Giving her his back, he groused, "Damn fickle woman."

Dr. Rupert ignored them both. He lowered the sheet just enough to slip his stethoscope inside. He listened, frowned, moved it, listened again, and frowned some more.

When he finished, he pulled the sheet back up to her chin. "Where's her medical history?"

Axel turned back around and handed it to him. The good doctor asked some questions, nodded in that doctorly fashion typical of his vocation, and finally said, "Well, I'm certain you have pneumonia, but we need X-rays, of course. Axel, you can bring her to my office first thing tomorrow for that. Say eight o'clock, before my regular schedule begins. Given how fast this came on her, I'd say it's likely bacterial, so I'm going to go ahead and give her a shot of antibiotic tonight. Are you allergic to anything, Miss Preston?"

"Call me Libby, and no." She didn't want a shot. She wanted to sleep.

"All right, Libby. And you can call me Cary. If you're going to be seeing Axel, I suppose we should all be friends."

"I'm not seeing him."

"No?"

Axel sounded like a bear when he growled, "She'll be seeing me."

Cary hid a smile. "You'll need plenty of bed rest, at least until your temperature returns to normal. Lots of fluids. At least six to eight glasses a day." He turned to Axel. "You'll see to it?"

"Yeah."

Libby's mouth fell open, which caused her to start coughing. Dr. Rupert helped to elevate her until she could catch her breath. Wheezing, she said, "I don't need his help."

Axel folded his arms over his chest. "Yes, you do."

"No—"

"Be gracious, Libby," Cary told her, and then went on before she could argue further. "Acetaminophen or ibuprofen to help control pain and fever. And use a cool mist humidifier or vaporizer to increase air moisture. It'll make it easier for you to breathe. Cool mist, Libby, not steam, understand?"

She bit her lower lip. "I don't have a cool mist humidifier and I don't have any medicine—"

"I'll run out," Axel told her. "The department store is open all night."

It wasn't to be borne. "You said you're a selfish bastard! Why don't you just leave?"

Cary drew back. "You told her?"

"Ha ha," Axel said. And as Libby groaned, drained from her outburst and hacking again, he said, "You got anything you can give her now for the fever? I hate for her to have to wait for me to shop."

Despite his concern for her, Cary seemed to be thoroughly enjoying himself. "Sure." He dug in his magical bag and produced two white pills. Axel hustled to get a glass of water, then lifted her with an arm behind her back and supported her while she drank.

He eased her back down. "Give her the shot, and I'll walk out with you."

Cary was already preparing the injection. He

gave her an apologetic look. "In the hip, Libby. Can you turn to your side for me?"

She looked at Axel, who rolled his eyes. "Right, I know. Turn my back so your delicate sensibilities won't be lacerated."

Cary waited while she adjusted the sheet the best she could, trying to show the least amount of skin. "This will sting," he told her, but truthfully she barely felt it above the rest of her miseries.

She thanked him for his help, and he patted her shoulder. "I'll see you tomorrow."

As the men prepared to leave, she curled in on herself and wallowed in self-pity. Why did she have to get sick now? She'd only just met Axel, and odds were after seeing what a fun date she could be, he'd never return. And she had graduation in a few weeks. The timing couldn't have been worse.

She didn't realize Axel was close until he brushed his knuckles across her cheek. "I'll be back within an hour. I took your keys off the kitchen counter, so I'll let myself in. Just try to sleep, okay?"

He'd taken her keys? How presumptuous. Eyes narrowed, she whispered, "Axel?"

His smile was very warm and tender. "Hmm?"

Libby gave up. "Thank you."

He searched her face, nodded, and finally took himself off. Sometime later, Libby became aware of him beside her in the bed. He tilted a glass to her lips and she drank it all, but declined when he offered to help her to the bathroom. She only wanted to sleep.

He lay down with her, once again naked, and spooned against her back. His lips touched her ear. "The vaporizer is on. I'm going to wake you in a few hours to take more medicine. Let me know if you need anything else."

Libby nodded, but one thought filled her mind: for a self-proclaimed selfish pig, he was more giving and caring than anyone she'd ever met.

She was the most pig-headed, obstinate woman he'd ever met. "You are *not* going to work, Libby. Jesus, you still have a fever. You can't take two steps without looking ready to collapse. I figured you to be a smart girl, so why are you talking so dumb?"

She sat huddled on the passenger side of his car on their return ride from Cary's office, where her pneumonia had been confirmed—not that there'd been any doubts.

Her hair was lank, her face ashen, her lips shivering. Wearing baggy sweats and a blanket, she looked like a drowning victim barely hanging onto life.

"My uncle will be furious if I don't show up."

For most of the previous night, Axel had wondered how he would keep his involvement with Libby—and he *was* involved—private from her pain-in-the-ass, all-too-important relative. But at that moment, he decided he didn't give a damn. "Let him be mad. I'll call him. I'll tell him you're ill. If he doesn't like it, tough shit."

With an expression of death, she peered at him. "Don't be an idiot. You can't call Uncle Elwood. He'll want to know what you have to do with anything."

Axel pulled into the parking lot. He needed to get her back in bed. "So I'll tell him."

"Tell him what?"

"That his niece is the sexiest piece of ass I've had in ages."

Libby almost slid to the floor of the car with a hard, cough-inducing gasp. "You *can't*—"

"Just kidding." He put the car in park and circled around to her side to open her door. "But it's true." As he scooped her up, she put her face in his neck. "You are a seriously sexy piece of work." He smiled.

She moaned. "Yeah, sweaty, hacking broads with chronic coughs really turn you on."

"*You* turn me on." And it didn't seem to matter that at the moment, sex was the farthest thing from his mind. He carried her up to her dinky apartment, enjoying the opportunity to show off his strength and play the gallant. He kicked the door shut. "Are you hungry?"

"No."

"How about soup anyway?"

"How about a nap?"

"After the soup."

And so it went. Everything he suggested, she argued about. She was the worst patient he'd ever had. And still, for some unfathomable reason, he enjoyed being with her.

After he force-fed her half a bowl of chicken noodle broth and she looked more asleep than awake, he broke the news. "I'm going to call Elwood now."

Her eyes snapped open. "Don't do this to me, Axel."

"To you? I'm the one who'll probably be kicked out of the hospital."

"You just don't know."

Such a desolate voice. He sat beside her and took her hands. "So tell me." Weariness etched her face, and he wanted to hold her again. But first things first. "Come on, Libby. Spill it. What awful things could Elwood possibly do to you? Will he have you blackballed from the hospital? Make you relocate to Alaska to find work? What?"

She turned her face away and her voice went flat. "He can tell me, again, that I'm just like my mother."

Keeping his tone gentle, Axel prompted, "How's that?"

"I look like her, and I suppose in a lot of ways I have her outlook on life."

"I take it she was a hard-working, independent, stubborn woman, too?" Axel teased.

She actually laughed, relaxing a little. "I don't remember much about her being stubborn, but yeah, she was independent. Elwood was her much older brother and they used to be close. But when he didn't accept or support her choices, she ignored him. See, Elwood is all seriousness and ambition, and my mother just enjoyed life. She didn't need fancy cars or jewelry or a big house. She used to tell me all she needed to be happy was me."

"A smart woman."

Libby looked at him, and a half smile curled

her pale lips. "Elwood hated it that Mom got pregnant by a car mechanic who took off the moment he knew I was on the way. Sometimes I think he hated me. But Mom told me it was just that he had to work long hours and didn't have time to visit very often."

Her eyes, her smile, were very soft when speaking of her mother. It was easy to see she'd been well loved, and had given a lot of love in return.

"Doctors are always on call," Axel told her, for the first time wondering what a woman would think of his own hectic schedule. "How do you feel about that?"

She gave it serious thought. "When someone's health, maybe even a life, hangs in the balance, of course doctors have to help when they can. But Elwood doesn't really care about people. He only cares about his reputation and the respect he gets."

Axel didn't want to insult her uncle again, so he let that go. "Not all doctors are like that."

She covered a yawn before saying, "I know that. I wouldn't want to be a nurse if I didn't respect the medical profession."

Leaving her apartment for the X-rays had really worn her out. Axel knew he should let her sleep, but first . . . "How did your mother die?"

Sadness clouded her eyes and she withdrew from him. "I wanted to swim, but Elwood wouldn't let us use his pool. So Mom took me to the river. She was out too far, flirting with some guys . . . and a boat went out of control." She shook her head and began to cough. "She drowned."

Axel pulled her upright and held her against

his shoulder, rubbing her back, wishing he hadn't brought it up. "I'm sorry." He kissed her ear, her cheek. "Shhh. Here, take a small drink."

When she'd regained her breath, she gave him a level, too serious look. "So you see, you can't let my uncle know that I was with you."

Insult mixed with exasperation. "Libby, no offense intended, but I'm not a mechanic. Elwood blusters a lot, but he respects me. Twenty years ago, when he was still my age, he was in the same position as me. It doesn't matter what my personal reputation might be."

"You mean your reputation as a 'me first' male slut?" She shook her head. "Forget it, Axel. I'm not buying that anymore, not with the way you enjoy playing nursemaid." And she tacked on, almost absently, "Not since my mother's death has anyone pampered me. Selfish, egotistic people don't do that."

Axel paid no attention to her, unsure whether she was complaining or complimenting. "Even sick, you're good company. But what I mean is that my professional reputation is rock solid."

"I never doubted it."

"Good. Then you should realize that Elwood would probably be pleased to know—"

Her raspy laugh interrupted his diatribe, and didn't sound the least bit nice. "What? That you're having a brief, purely sexual fling with his niece? Yeah, that'd thrill him."

It definitely wasn't just sexual, not on his part, and Axel wasn't sure he wanted it to be so damn brief either. After only one night—which usually was enough to satisfy him—he couldn't even begin to think of walking away from her. He'd meant what he said: she was good company. She didn't complain, she didn't simper or put on airs. She was herself at all times, friendly, funny, independent, serious, sexy, and giving. He liked her. A lot.

He maybe even more than liked her.

But he could hardly start declaring himself yet. "What we do sexually is none of Elwood's business. You're a grown woman, or so you keep insisting."

"Start up on my age again," she warned, "and sick or not, I'll get up and kick your butt."

Axel grinned, knowing she'd try, and knowing he'd enjoy her efforts if she wasn't sick. "No need to tax yourself. Believe me, I know you're a woman." He propped his hands on his hips, attempting to look stern. "But woman or not, you're still too ill to go to work."

She rolled to her side and groaned. "I know. I feel like crap." She held out a hand. "Could you give me my phone?"

He didn't want to. The urge to protect her was almost worse than the urge to hold her. And the urge to make love to her. "All right." He held it out of her reach. "But don't grovel. Don't apologize. Give him the facts and let him deal with them any way he wants."

She snatched the phone away from him and made the call. Axel kept close, deliberately listening in, frowning when she repeated, for the

third time, that she was just plain too sick to
work.

When she finally hung up, he said, "I take it
he wasn't pleased?"

"He threatened to drop in on me, to make
sure I'm okay." That made her shudder. "A first
for Uncle Elwood. Then again, I've never called
in sick before." With a long sigh, she sank into
her pillow. "Now go home so I can sleep."

Axel had no intention of leaving just yet. He
took her dirty dishes to the kitchen, refilled the
humidifier, checked in with his answering service, and then made a few necessary calls. Basically, he bided his time till she woke again. Then
he helped her bathe—a distinct pleasure—
made her eat again, and even napped with her.

Given his history and usual preferences, it
made no sense how even the mundane with her
seemed special. Napping? He snorted to himself. If anyone found out, he'd never live it
down. But being beside her, feeling her body
snuggled in with his, filled him with contentment.

By the following day, thanks to the antibiotics
and his excellent care, she felt much more
human. He helped her do some studying, then
rented several movies and sat with her in the
bed, sharing meals, laughing a little, and just
plain enjoying a woman's company.

It was weird. It was relaxing. Axel thought it
might not bode well for his bachelor status. But
finally, by Sunday, he'd accepted the inevitable.

He knew he'd been caught—hook, line, and
sinker. Only problem was, did she feel the same?

Chapter Seven

After the strangest weekend of her life, Monday should have been comforting, a return to the familiar. Once again Libby had her space to herself. There was no naked man to bump into, no one hovering over her or monitoring her every move. No one fretting, no one holding her, kissing her nose and forehead and ear. No one making her wish she was well so she could take advantage of the proximity of that hulking, muscular, totally male bod.

But instead, it felt odd to have the place to herself, and worse than that, she felt . . . empty. How had she gotten used to him so quickly?

And how would she handle it if she never got to see him again?

Pining over her circumstances was just plain dumb. Axel was still a doctor, which meant he had patients to see, women who depended on him for a lot more than she did.

And against his wishes, she had classes she couldn't miss. Graduation was just around the bend, with plenty of exams to take between now and then.

She told herself it'd be wise to relegate the weekend as an aberration, an event never to occur again. If Axel called, and that was doubtful given what a pill she'd been, she'd be blasé about it. She'd resort to their original agreement of a fling. And flings did not include exclusivity or duty calls.

By the time she got home from school, she was again as limp as a used dishcloth, ready to nap, and determined on her course.

She checked the answering machine first thing. No messages. So . . . he hadn't called.

Deflated, despite the lecture she'd given herself again and again throughout the long day, Libby pulled off her jacket, kicked off her shoes, and flopped down on the bed to stare up at the ceiling. She should eat something. Take her medicine. Maybe do some studying.

But she was still there, half asleep and in the same position where she'd landed, when a knock sounded on her door.

Startled, she sat up, and ridiculous girlish hope swelled her heart. Before she could leave the bed, a key scraped in the lock and Axel pushed the door open. Libby blinked at him in mute surprise.

"Hey." He smiled at her, shut the door. "How do you feel?"

"Uh . . ."

He approached her with wary indifference, tossed a suit coat onto the back of the loveseat, and loosened his tie. "Have you eaten?"

Even for Axel, keeping her key to come and go as he pleased was outrageous. She tried to think of some way to berate him, but he looked really, really good in a tie and five o'clock shadow, and that distracted her. "No."

"Got plans for the evening?"

She shook her head, unsure of his intent, still ripe with hopefulness. "Studying to do. That's all." She noticed that he dropped the key back into his pants pocket. "You planning to keep that?"

He met her gaze with a searing challenge. "Did you want it back?"

She tried to answer, but she couldn't come up with anything intelligent. She should say yes, but her heart said, *Keep it, visit whenever you want, stay a while.*

Deciding to get things out in the open, Libby sighed. "I just . . . I don't know what we're doing here."

Another smile, this one full of sensual promise, gave her half an answer. "You agreed to a torrid sex affair, remember?"

She remembered. "What does that have to do with my key?"

"You don't want anyone to know we're seeing each other, so coming here is safer than using my place." He cocked a brow. "I figure sooner or later you'll be recovered enough to appease my lust—"

She opened her mouth to agree, and he said, "But not today." He gave her a quick once-over, then tsked. "You look wiped out."

With him opening the top button on his dress shirt and rolling up his sleeves, her recovery seemed to be happening at an alarming rate. "It was a long day."

"You should still be in bed." As if by rote, he went to her kitchen and got her a tall glass of iced tea and her medicine. He carried it to her. "How about we shower, order a pizza, and then just relax?"

Shower with Axel? Now that had promise.

"You don't have anything more important to do?"

Her question made him defensive. "I can be as lazy and self-indulgent here with you as I can at my own place."

"You aren't . . . seeing anyone else who would be more fun?"

A new seriousness entered his gaze. "One woman at a time, Libby. And right now, I'm anticipating what we'll do once you've recouped."

Wow, he made that sound so promising. "Being sick sucks." She washed down her antibiotic and two aspirin with one long gulp.

"I can make you feel better."

He was *such* a temptation, and she hated disappointing him. "Sorry, Axel. The soul is willing, anxious even, but the energy level is just kaput."

Axel caught both her hands and pulled her to her feet. "Come on. You'll be more comfortable after a shower."

She groaned.

"I'll do all the work." He began backing toward her bathroom, tugging her along. "You can just stand under the spray and let me soap you." His voice dropped. "And rinse you."

Libby felt a wave of heat that had nothing to do with illness and everything to do with Dr. Axel Dean. "This is so unfair."

Smiling at her flushed cheeks, he whispered, "And dry you."

Disgruntled, she stood docile while he undressed her. "I was supposed to get a turn touching you."

His fingers froze on the snap to her slacks. "Yeah, well, we'll save that for when you're 100 percent again. Today is just my time to play."

Going to one knee, he pulled down her pants and kissed her belly. "You'll enjoy yourself, I promise. And then you can nap while I get food together."

Libby stroked her fingers through his dark hair. "For a selfish bastard, you're pretty good at giving."

Putting both hands into the back of her panties and sliding them down, he said, "In this instance, giving is also taking. Now hush."

After he had her naked, he stepped back and eyed her from head to toe. With one trembling hand, he cupped her right breast. "The things you do to me, woman." He shook his head, then turned to start the shower. Libby leaned against the wall, eyes closed, legs weak.

When Axel slipped his arm around her waist,

she opened her eyes again to be greeted with his now familiar nudity. "You realize this is the equivalent of tormenting a diabetic with a basketful of sweet treats?"

His smile quirked. "I'm salty, not sweet." He pressed a warm, gentle kiss to her mouth and lifted her into the shower with him. "Now just relax."

"I already know this is going to be torture."

"For me, sweetheart. Never for you."

Libby didn't understand what he meant by that, and a few minutes later, after Axel's slick, soapy hands had been all over her body, she no longer cared.

"Axel?" she moaned, leaning into him while his fingers slipped over and around her nipples, teasing, driving her crazy.

"Let me rinse you," he whispered, and he turned her to face the spray, bracing her with his body at her back. The warm water washed over her, and still his hands were on her, over her breasts, her belly, and down between her legs.

"No," she whimpered, so weak she wasn't sure she could stay on her feet. "No more."

"Shhh. Trust me." He held her upright with one arm around her rib cage, just beneath her breasts. With the other, he parted her sex, stroking, delving.

Libby pressed her head back against his shoulder. Her breath stuttered, her muscles tightened.

Two thick fingers pressed into her, making her cry out with the wonderful sensation.

"You see?" he murmured in satisfaction, and then his thumb was on her clitoris, moving back and forth while his fingers pressed, retreated, pressed again. His open mouth moved along her throat and shoulder, the water cascaded over her breasts, and she felt the orgasm building, stronger and stronger.

She cried out again, her fingers clamping down on his hard thighs, her legs stiffening.

He supported her, held her, pushed her completely over the edge, and when she went limp, he eased his fingers out of her and turned her into his body. "Damn, you are so beautiful."

Libby felt herself fading away. She'd been mush before the orgasm, but now her legs actually felt numb and staying awake seemed more trouble than it was worth. "Sorry," she mumbled, letting the fatigue take her.

"Sleep, baby. I've got you."

He turned the water off and Libby was only vaguely aware of being wrapped in a towel and carried to the bed.

Over an hour later, she awoke to find Axel sitting in a chair near the bed, fully dressed, eating pizza and watching her. Her hair was still damp, spread out around her, and she sluggishly pushed up to one elbow.

As if he hadn't been sitting there staring at her, watching her sleep, he got up and fetched a slice of pizza and a cola. He handed them to her. "Hungry?"

"Humiliated," she replied, moving to sit up so she could eat. "I keep passing out on you."

With an odd sort of affection that had nothing to do with sex, he ruffled her hair. "You need your rest."

After a big bite of cold pizza, Libby eyed him. She didn't understand him and the things he did. "And what do you need?"

"Nothing that can't wait." He winked and picked up his suit coat. "I have rounds at the hospital early tomorrow, so I'm going to head out and get some sleep. When you finish eating, take your meds again, okay?"

"And here you told me that you didn't see me as a patient."

"I don't." He bent, stroked her bottom lip with his thumb, and kissed her. "I see you as a woman I want, and I can't have you till you're well. So help me out here and do what you can to recover good health, okay?"

Put that way . . . "I promise to follow doctor's orders to the letter."

"That's the spirit."

She caught his hand before he could leave her. "Axel?"

He raised a brow.

"You do realize that you're ruining your reputation as a bad boy bent on his own pleasure, right?"

He cupped her face and kissed her again. "Maybe it's time I got a new reputation."

He left before Libby could question him on that.

Axel thought he'd figured out a very nice plan of attack. For the fourth day in a row, he'd taken care of her, tending her health, her body, and her sexual needs.

He'd confused her, no doubt about that. But his goal was to get her addicted to him, so slowly that she might not even notice.

He'd enjoyed himself, but he didn't think he could take too much more. She was so cute when she felt helpless, so surly in her struggle for complete independence—and so sensually honest in her physical satisfaction.

He liked everything about her, even her purple toenails and her tendency to insult him. He especially liked the way she came, how she made those sexy, carnal sounds deep in her throat and how she clutched at him—as if she never wanted to let him go.

The weekend was fast approaching again and he wanted to spend it in bed, making love to Libby. She no longer had any fever, and other than the dragging fatigue typical of pneumonia, she seemed her old self again.

Not that he really knew her old self since each and every day he learned something new about her. Eventually, he wanted to know all her secrets.

"Daydreaming again?" Cary asked.

Axel looked up from his desk. He'd finished his paperwork an hour ago. "You here for Nora?"

"Actually, Nora left a while ago. She's going shopping with Frances."

Frances was his sister-in-law, the woman who'd made his brother Booker a very happy man. "I didn't hear her leave."

"I know. Like I said, you were daydreaming."
Cary folded his arms and leaned in the doorway. Since his office was in the same building
complex as Axel's, they often met up after work.
"Want to have a drink or something?"

Axel glanced at his watch and pushed back
his chair. "If we make it quick. Libby should be
getting home in about an hour."

"Home?"

"Her place." Axel removed his white coat and
hung it on the peg behind him. "Can't take her
to my place because she still doesn't want anyone to know she's seeing me."

They walked out together, pausing for Axel to
lock up.

"Now there's a twist," Cary remarked. "Usually you're the one dodging things, trying to
make certain it doesn't get too serious."

"She's not dodging." God, he hoped she wasn't.
Axel hated to think he'd be falling for a woman
who didn't want him. "It's her uncle. He gives her
a hard time over everything."

"So you're . . . what? Just keeping it quiet
until it—whatever *it* is—runs its course?"

"No." Axel frowned. "I'm . . . I don't know
yet. Things got out of whack with her being sick
and everything. I'm sort of feeling my way right
now."

"But it will run its course, right?"

Axel snorted. "What's with the it talk?"

"Okay." Cary stopped as they reached their
cars. "You name it."

Axel stared at him, blank-brained. "Why does it need a name, damn it? We're involved. End of story."

"*Secretly* involved."

"So?"

Cary held up both hands. "So nothing. It's just unusual for you to get involved, secretly or otherwise."

Axel had the awful suspicion that it was more unusual for Libby. "She's different."

"I know. Everything you claimed not to want."

Was Cary deliberately baiting him? Axel slanted him an evil look. "What the hell is that supposed to mean?"

"Young?" Cary held up one finger after another. "Sweet. Serious. Not really all that . . . stacked."

"Get your hand out of my face." Axel unlocked his BMW and opened the door. Behind him, he could practically feel Cary snickering. "She's young, no denying that. But she's also mature. And if you think she's sweet, then you haven't heard her insulting me with inexhaustible energy."

"She insults you, huh? Well then, that's another for the list."

"And yeah," Axel said, taking an aggressive stance. "She's serious, but she's also damn funny. And just because she's not top heavy doesn't mean I can't be attracted to her."

Again, Cary held up his hands in the universal sign of surrender. "Hey, I think she's really cute. And she has great legs."

Axel's hair damn near stood on end with that jibe. "Just when in the hell were you looking at her legs?"

This time, Cary laughed outright. He took in Axel's deadly frown and laughed some more. Slapping him on the back, he said, "Damn Axel, you've got it bad. I remember a time—not that long ago, mind you—when you'd have been listing the attributes of any conquest. But this time, I'm not supposed to notice that the girl has legs? Whipped. That's what you are. Totally whipped."

Axel took a mean step toward him, but Cary defused his temper with a smile. "Go home to the girl. Profess undying love. But do me a favor, okay? Try not to hurt her. Whether she insults you or not, she's still sweet and I'd hate to think of her ever crying over you."

Feeling lost at sea, Axel watched as his best friend strode away whistling, a married man without a care. Maybe marriage did that for you, put everything in perspective because, really, if you had the right woman waiting for you, what else mattered?

It was a question Axel had asked himself a few times since his brother and his best friend had both hitched up. But never before had he wondered in such a personal way, as if his own happiness hinged on the answer.

No, he would never make Libby cry, and he'd punch out any guy who did, maybe even including her uncle. He was jealous. And possessive. And making love to her was the most exciting thing he'd ever experienced, but he also enjoyed just plain being with her.

He considered the ramifications of his situation all the way to her apartment. Unfortunately for her, he'd worked himself into quite a state by the time he arrived, and she was there in the kitchen making dinner.

For the two of them.

Like they were some happily married couple or something.

Axel stormed in, took one look at her, and wanted her with a need so violent, he shook. She didn't look overly tired, her fever was long gone, and she actually smiled.

"Dinner will be ready in a minute," she said, oblivious to his mood.

Axel shrugged out of his suit coat and let it drop.

Libby didn't look up as she closed the oven door. "Pork chops, baked potatoes, and salad. I hope that's okay."

Axel yanked his tie free, unbuttoned his dress shirt. It, too, got dropped.

"I even picked up a lemon meringue pie for dessert."

He kicked off his shoes, unbuckled his belt— and Libby glanced up.

Her eyes widened. "What are you doing?"

"Take your clothes off," he ordered. He stepped up close to her, reached around her, and turned off the oven.

Libby glanced sideways at the oven dial. "I suppose the food will keep."

Axel shoved his pants down, taking his boxers and socks off at the same time. "You'll like it hard and fast, babe. I promise." He fished a condom from his wallet and tore it open with his teeth.

Lips parting, eyes going heavy, Libby whispered, "Okay."

She wasn't going fast enough to suit him, so he whisked her long-sleeved T off over her head and with one hand opened the front clasp on her bra.

Catching her under the arms, he lifted her and fastened his mouth on one tender nipple.

Stiffening at the shock of it, then softening in immediate acceptance, Libby moaned and tangled her fingers in his hair. "Axel."

Still holding her like that, he walked them both to the bed and tumbled her onto it. He straightened, opened her pants, and stripped them off her. "Sorry. I know you've only just recovered, but I've wanted you too much for too long to be patient."

She opened her arms and her legs to him. "I want you, too."

Damn. Axel rolled on the condom and came down over her, kissing her hard, taking her mouth with demand while letting his hands roam everywhere. He caressed her, stroked, sought out all the hot, humid places on her body, and less than a minute later, with two fingers pressed deep inside her and her anxious, panting breaths on his shoulder, he knew she was ready enough.

Slowly, he pulled his fingers out, trailing them up and over her turgid clitoris. She groaned out loud, her whole body clenching in reaction. Unwilling to wait a second more, Axel slipped his arms under her thighs, caught her knees in the crook of his elbows, and spread her wide. His gaze holding hers, he told her, "It's deeper this way," and he pushed the broad head of his penis into her with a long, low groan.

She was tight, but wet, making the way easy.

Lost in her pleasure, her slender legs strained against his hold, but Axel had a hundred pounds on her and easily controlled her. By small degrees, he sank in, pulled back, sank in again, each time giving her another inch, each time relishing her aching moans and gasping breaths and the bite of her sharp nails on his shoulders.

Her back arched, inadvertently giving him better access.

Axel felt her clamping tight around his cock, felt the soft, slick giving of her body, felt himself touching against her womb, and he almost lost it.

He looked at her face, twisted with exquisite need, her teeth sunk into her bottom lip, and he had to lock his jaw to hold back. But more than his own release, he wanted hers, he wanted to see her come, to know she belonged to him.

As he leaned into her, thrusting harder, faster, her thighs pressed into her breasts and she went wild, crying out, struggling to match his rhythm, and then she was coming, her movements suspended, her breath held for a beat before she exhaled on a long, shuddering, high-pitched moan of surrender.

Axel never once closed his eyes because looking at her, seeing her beneath him, made it that much better.

When she was spent, he carefully freed her legs and rested atop her, enjoying the beat of her heart against his.

She stroked his back with an idle hand. "You didn't . . . ?"

"No, I didn't."

"Why?"

Because he didn't want it to end. Ever. "I want it to last a while longer."

"Oh." Then she whispered, "You were wrong."

His own lust unappeased, Axel could barely breathe, much less think. "About?"

"Liking it hard."

"I felt you come, Libby."

"Mmmm." She gave him a brief hug. "But I don't just like it. I *love* it fast and hard."

He turned his face in and kissed her throat, before lifting to his elbows to look at her. "What else do you love?"

She nuzzled him, inhaling, breathing him in. "The way you smell after sex, all hot and male."

His big hand slid into her silky hair. "Anything else?"

"I especially love feeling you on top of me."

Axel stared into her blue eyes with his heart full and his body taut. Slowly, he pulled back, then just as slowly, he sank in again. "Do you love this?"

Her chest expanded on a breath. "Yes."

"And this?" He slid one hand beneath her bottom, arching her pelvis up to accept his next thrust.

"That . . . ah, that, too."

Maintaining a leisurely pace, he kissed his

way from her lips to her throat to her breast. "This?" And he suckled on a ripe nipple, tonguing her, leaving her wet and tight and hot.

"*Yessss.*"

Suddenly he clamped down, sucking hard, thrusting harder. "Tell me," he said, briefly lifting his head, his fingers digging into her tender flesh. "Tell me you love this, too."

"*Axel.*"

The way she called his name set him off, and he started coming. Too soon, he thought, but he couldn't pull back, couldn't measure his strokes or his intensity, couldn't make it last any longer. As the release rolled through him, his tension ebbed, draining him, stealing his strength. He slumped onto her.

"Oh God," she groaned, then laughed softly. "That was . . . amazing."

Heart still thundering, as if it wanted to break free of his chest, Axel asked, "You loved it?"

"I did."

He swallowed hard, squeezed in closer to her. "Do you love me?"

Chapter Eight

Libby froze, her hands flat on his back, her legs around him.

Axel rose up enough to see the fear in her eyes, the paleness of her cheeks. It didn't matter. He just plain didn't give a damn.

"Because I love you." He was still inside her, a part of her, and never before had that carried so much meaning. What if she was as cavalier about sex as he'd always been? What if she didn't feel the special closeness now, closeness so precious that it choked him up and put him in knots?

He struggled to find the words. "I love making love to you, and sleeping with you." He pushed her hair back from her face with both hands. "I love talking to you and just being with you."

Time passed, and with each second of heavy silence, Axel grew more rigid.

"Maybe . . ." She cleared her throat, looking trapped. "Maybe you just think you do because things have been weird."

"Weird how?" He wouldn't move until he got the answer he wanted.

"I've been sick and you've felt responsible for me."

"No, I took responsibility because, sick or not, I wanted to be with you."

"You're used to lots of sex."

He shrugged. He couldn't deny liking sex, and true, he seldom had to go for long without it. "With you, it's different."

"You get what you want from a woman," she accused, "and then you get over her and move on. But you haven't been able to get what you want from me . . ."

"Of course not. Because I want everything from you."

She started breathing too fast. "You want sex. You said so yourself."

"I'm not an idiot, Libby. I know the difference between what I feel now and what I've felt with other women. If you don't love me, I'll work on you. I'll somehow get you to change your mind. But don't think I'm an idiot."

"I wouldn't!" She smacked his shoulder. "I don't. You're the most . . . well, remarkable man I've ever met."

It was a start. "Remarkable, huh? But you don't love me?"

"I don't know."

The words cut deep, but he still smiled. "You don't have to worry that I'll interfere with your plans or make your life difficult. I know you have priorities, and right now graduating is at the top of the list." She started to say something and Axel hushed her. "It's okay."

He moved up and away from her, going into the bathroom to remove the condom, to splash cold water on his face, and get his thoughts in order. Talk about getting off track. He could hardly sneak his way into her life if he went around blurting out frigging love sonnets. Jesus.

By the time he left the bathroom, Libby was sitting on the side of the bed, the sheet around her.

"Here's what we'll do." Axel pulled her upright and removed the sheet. "First, don't ever hide from me. Whether we're in agreement or not, modesty between us is ridiculous."

Her chin went up. "I wasn't hiding."

"Good." Damn, she was cute when riled. "You feel fully recovered?"

"Yes."

He knew she still suffered some fatigue, but he wouldn't debate it with her. "So there's no reason I can't get my fill of you now, is there?"

Suspicion, maybe a little worry, edged into her expression. "I suppose not."

Axel bent and kissed her. "Then let's see how long that takes. If by the time you graduate we're both still interested, we'll tell your uncle about us. Agreed?"

Her brows shot up and she laughed nervously. "Believe me, Axel, Elwood won't like the idea any more in two weeks than he will right now."

Axel stared her straight in her beautiful blue

eyes and said, "If I tell him we're getting married, he won't object."

Libby's mouth opened. Her lips moved, but nothing came out.

Not even an objection.

Grinning, knowing he had her, Axel said, "Now, did you say pork chops? My favorite. And I think I've worked up an appetite, so let's eat."

With Axel at her side, his hand on her waist, Libby stared at her uncle in complete stupefaction. "Come again?"

Elwood harrumphed and blustered. Libby knew he wanted a private word with her, and she knew he didn't understand why Dr. Axel Dean loomed so close. But it seemed he had something more important to discuss with her first. And besides, Axel looked as stubborn as a mule, glued to the floor, unwilling to budge a single inch.

She was used to that, though. Since that day he'd declared himself, he'd shown her in a hundred different ways that he cared. Being with her now, during her graduation, was only expected.

Having Uncle Elwood approach was not.

"I said I'm proud of you."

Axel's frown eased away and he nodded. "About time."

Elwood glared at him. Usually a glare from the chief of staff sent doctors scurrying. Axel just pulled Libby closer as if to dare Elwood to question him.

Since her return to good health, Axel had been glutting himself.

He was such a sexual man, he probably defied the record books, being ready day, night, and sometimes in between, when their schedules allowed. It seemed the more they made love, the more he wanted to make love.

And variety . . . Lord have mercy, the man loved variety. He'd taken her in the shower, in the kitchen, on the bed, beside the bed . . . Libby sighed. Before they left for her graduation service, just to make his point, he'd hoisted up her long gown and made love to her against the wall with a tenderness that had her floating through the ceremony.

But it went beyond the sex. Axel talked with her, watched movies with her, slept beside her and held her close and touched her for no apparent reason other than that he enjoyed the feel of her hair, her skin, her palm to his, her heartbeat mingling with his own.

After years of planning and, more recently, weeks of study, she'd completed her education. It should have been a monumental moment. But truthfully, her priorities had changed since meeting one very sexy doctor. Her education and independence were still important to her, but they weren't nearly as important as Axel. He'd become so enmeshed in her life, she couldn't imagine the days without him. She wanted to marry him and be with him forever. She wanted him to tell her again that he loved her.

But she didn't want him coerced. And if he kept acting so familiar with her, her uncle would catch on and then he'd be making demands and issuing insults, and Axel's career could be threatened.

Axel had to know it, too, but he didn't seem the least bit concerned.

"I know I haven't been very supportive." Elwood rubbed the back of his neck, showing an uncommon uneasiness that almost made Libby feel sympathetic. "I've told you many times that you're like your mother. And in so many ways, you are."

Axel's hand tightened on her waist. "I hope you mean smart, beautiful, and ambitious."

Elwood nodded, but spoke directly to Libby. "Not only do you look like her, but you're as vivacious, as outspoken and witty and strong as she ever was. I loved your mother, Libby, and it destroyed me that she didn't show better judgment with men. She let herself be used, and in the end it—"

"That's enough." No matter what, Libby wouldn't let him insult her mother.

Elwood stiffened. "I'm sorry. I know you feel defensive of her. What I'm trying to say is that you have all your mother's better qualities, with none of her weaknesses."

Libby wasn't in the least complimented. "Enjoying life isn't a weakness, Uncle Elwood."

"It is when you allow it to damage your future and your reputation."

Axel heaved a sigh. "I think you two are at cross purposes here. Elwood, why don't you just spit it out?"

Libby said, "Be quiet, Axel," and that seemed

to stun her uncle. Especially when Axel just gave her a smart salute. But she'd already learned that Axel didn't get insulted easily. Oh, if he thought he was in the right he'd argue her into the ground, but he had the good sense to know when to back off.

And sometimes he had the good sense to divert her with a kiss. Or a touch.

He always supported her. And God, she loved him for it.

Bringing her mind back to her uncle, Libby curled her lip. "I know my illegitimacy is a tough pill for an esteemed man like yourself to swallow."

"That's not what I mean at all." Appearing more flustered by the moment, Elwood clasped his hands behind his back and cast a nervous glance at Axel. "You were a gift to your mother, and I had hoped the responsibility of a child would make her settle down. But until the day she died, she showed no moderation with men. It was flirting with strangers that got her killed that day on the river, and I've blamed myself forever."

Libby felt her jaw drop. "Why in the world would you blame yourself?"

"If I'd let you both come to my pool that day . . ."

Incredibly, Libby softened. "It's old news, Uncle Elwood." She even touched his arm, offering the only consolation she could. "Like you said, Mom enjoyed male company. You can't blame yourself for her actions. But please don't judge me by them either. I've never chased after men, or made them a priority in my life."

Axel cleared his throat. "I can vouch for that. No chasing from Libby."

Elwood gave him another dirty look before facing Libby again. "I know that. You've been extremely levelheaded." He reached into his suit coat and pulled out a thick envelope. "From the moment you came to live with me, I was determined that you'd be different from her. I wanted you to be more responsible. I wanted you to live a long, full life."

Libby could only shake her head. So he'd only done what he thought was best for her—by alienating her? By making her feel unloved?

Elwood straightened his shoulders. "I could have easily given you everything, but I wanted you to earn what you got in the hope that it would mean more to you."

Axel stepped forward. "What about love, Elwood? How hard was she supposed to work for that?"

Libby couldn't believe Axel would go toe-to-toe with the chief of staff on her behalf.

Affronted, Elwood scowled darkly. "Just what do you have to do with any of this, Dean?"

Oh no, Libby thought, please don't tell him what you have to do with it! But one look at Axel's face and she knew the bomb was about to blow. "Axel," she said in warning, but it was too late.

"I love her." That statement landed with all the subtlety of a tsunami.

Hearing him say it again made Libby almost melt. Sure, he'd said it a few weeks ago, but after her protestations, he'd kept his feelings to himself. He'd shared everything else, his hands, his mouth, his affection and camaraderie, his time and attention, but he hadn't spoken words of love again.

"Axel?"

His fingers brushed her cheek. "What? You thought I'd changed my mind? Silly girl." And then to Elwood: "If I can talk her into it, I'm going to marry her."

Oh geez. Despite the many people milling around her, despite her uncle's bristling confusion, Libby focused only on Axel. "You still want to marry me?"

Now Axel scowled. "Of course I do. Elwood can blunder around all he wants trying to find the right words. But I already know them. You, Libby Preston, are a very special woman. Beautiful inside and out, strong but soft, determined but giving. I think I fell in love with you that very first night, at Elwood's party."

Elwood went rigid in indignation. "You've known her since then?"

Rolling his eyes, Axel said, "Oh, lighten up, Elwood. I just told you I love her, so what does it matter how long we've been associated?"

"It matters." Elwood turned a stony glare on Libby. "Do you love him?"

Talk about being put in the spotlight. Libby's cheeks warmed and her heart swelled. She hated spilling her guts in front of her uncle, but Axel looked very vulnerable as he waited to hear what she'd say, and she didn't have it in her to keep him in suspense. "Almost from that first moment I saw him."

A grin burst over Axel's face. "Damn, I'm glad to hear that."

Elwood went so far as to smile. "Then I suppose I'll need to come up with a wedding gift, as well." He handed her the envelope. "But this is for your graduation, for making me so very proud of you."

Libby took the envelope hesitantly. "What is it?"

"Every dime you've ever given me. The room and board, the college loans, everything. I've saved it all, from that very first summer job you got, and I've added a few thousand in."

"Oh no." Libby tried to hand it back to him. "I don't want this."

"Please." He folded his hands around hers, closing the envelope in her grasp. "For once, let me do what's right. I always intended to give the money back to you, you know. I took it in the first place as a way to teach you a lesson. I thought I'd be returning it with regrets. I thought I'd have a lecture to share on the weight of the world and the trials you'd face." He shook his head, saddened. "Now I realize that I've been your biggest trial. But you're strong enough, capable enough, to handle anything life brings you. You certainly don't need the money, but this is my way of trying to help you make a good start with your new career."

Numb, Libby kept the envelope and stared at her uncle.

"So," Axel said, "you won't object to us marrying? Not that I care, you understand, but I won't have you hurting Libby."

Libby rolled her eyes. "I can take care of myself."

Together, Axel and Elwood said, "Don't I know it."

With the exact words between them, they looked at each other in startled surprise, then laughed out loud.

When his chuckles had died down, Elwood wiped his eyes and said, "No objections at all. Just see that you treat her right." And he added, "Treat her better than I did."

"You can count on it."

After Elwood left, Axel pulled her close and kissed her. "Now, that went better than I thought."

Libby shook her head. "I suppose my uncle does respect you, because he didn't faint." She laid her palm on his chest and said, "Thank heavens I've graduated. That means I can put my mind to wedding plans."

With a devilish twinkle in his eyes, Axel said, "I thought Elwood's gardens might make the perfect place for the ceremony."

Libby choked. "The gardens!"

Axel pulled her close, kissed her nose, and whispered, "They have special meaning to me. And when I get you there this time, believe me, I'll say all the right things."

"Like?"

He cupped her face, all teasing gone. "Through sickness and in health, till death do us part."

"Oh." Grinning, Libby put her arms around him. "In that case, I agree, the gardens will be perfect."

If you enjoyed this collection about the Dean Brothers and their friend Cary, you won't want to miss *The Watson Brothers*, coming this May!

Please turn the page for an excerpt.

He knew that damned aggravating little giggle anywhere. It was throaty and pure and never failed to set him on edge. He'd listened to it every Sunday for two long months when Pete, his baby brother, had been infatuated with her. That giddy laugh was often directed at him, instead of Pete, as it should have been.

With a heavy dose of dread and a visible grimace, Sam Watson slewed his head away from his whiskey and toward that annoying twitter. Shit. Sure enough, there sat Ariel Mathers. At the bar no less. And there were two men chatting her up.

What the hell was she doing in this dive? He glanced around but didn't see his brother anywhere. As to that, no one particular man ap-

peared to be with her. Huh. The little twit was
slumming.

So many times since first meeting her, Sam
had wanted to put her over his knee. For lead-
ing his brother on at a time when he'd been
vulnerable. For flirting with him, Sam, a man
much too old for her. And especially for being so
damned adorable, he almost couldn't stand it.

And now this.

His palm itched at the thought of it and his
mind conjured the image of her over his knees,
her tush bared. He started to sweat, knowing
that if he had her in such a position, punish-
ment would be the very last thing on his mind.
She was so petite that her bottom would be
small. And pale. And no doubt silky soft . . .

Shit, shit, shit.

His eyes burned as he stared at her slim back.
She had her hair up with a few baby-fine blond
curls kissing her nape. Little gold hoops in her
earlobes glittered with the bar lights. The heart-
shaped tush he'd so often fantasized over, now
perched on a bar stool, was easily outlined beneath the clinging silk skirt of her dress.

At twenty-four she was twelve years too young
for him. His mind understood that. His dick
didn't care.

She paused in whatever nonsense she'd been
uttering to the hapless fool beside her. As she
started to look around, Sam twisted in his seat to
face the window. *Do* not *let her see me,* he prayed.
He waited, pretending to be drunk when he was
more alert than he'd ever been in his life. He'd
nursed one whiskey since coming into the bar,

but he'd pretended drunkenness on his way in. Anyone who noticed him would assume he was there to top off an already inebriated night.

Fifteen seconds ticked by, then thirty, a minute—no one approached him. Sam relaxed, but kept his face averted, just in case. No way could he carry off his assignment tonight if Ariel got in the way.

He should have known better than to stare at her. People felt that sort of thing, just as he'd felt the big bruiser at the far booth watching him. He would have liked to order another drink, to call further attention to his feigned drunkenness. But with Ariel sitting there, it would be too risky.

Better to get this over with now, before he did something stupid. Like staring at her again.

Opening his wallet to show the bloated contents—two hundred dollars' worth—he pulled out a ten-dollar tip. He laid it on the table, stumbled to his feet and staggered out the door.

Once outside, he deliberately started across the street toward the abandoned, shadowed building where he would supposedly retrace his path home—and where his backup could clearly see him. Sam took his time, singing a crude bawdy tune about a woman from Nantucket, who according to the men, liked to suck it. It was a favorite limerick from his youth and he knew it by heart, but this time he missed some words, slurred a few others.

He pitched into the brick wall, laughed too loud, and started off again, only to trip over a garbage can, causing an awful racket. He gave a rank curse, stepped in something disgusting that he didn't want to identify, and dropped up against the side of a broken, collapsible fire escape.

Sam was fumbling for a more upright position when a meaty paw grabbed his upper arm, filling him with satisfaction. The perp had taken the bait.

"Give me your wallet."

Jolting around, Sam acted surprised, then spat in the big chap's face, "Fug off."

A ham-sized fist hit him in the side of the head and he saw stars for real. Jesus, he hadn't expected the fellow to get nasty so quick. Most of the thefts in the area—and there'd been plenty of late—had been done without any real personal damage.

Across a six-block area that covered three bars in Duluth, Indiana, more than twelve muggings had taken place in less than a month. It wasn't the best part of the city, so muggings weren't uncommon. But twelve? And all against men carrying substantial amounts of money. That smacked of premeditated, organized activity, and grabbed the attention of the police.

Sam twisted away, but was brought back around for another punch, this one in the gut. He bent double and almost puked.

Because he knew the guys would never let him live it down, he managed to keep his supper in his belly where it belonged. Just barely.

Where the hell were they anyway? Taking their own sweet time?

Before Sam could decide to take another punch or sneak in one of his own, a female banshee cry split the air, making his ears ring and his hair stand on end. Two seconds later his perp got hit from behind by a small tornado and the momentum drove him straight into Sam, against the side of the metal stairs. It felt like his damn ribs cracked.

Everyone started struggling at once and they went down in a heap, Sam on the bottom so that his head and back hit the hard, gravel-covered ground with a jarring impact. The wind left his lungs in a whoosh.

While supine and wheezing, Sam got a good look at the familiar blond clinging tenaciously to his perp's hair with one hand while trying to use her purse like a club with the other. Sam couldn't quite tell if she was attempting to bludgeon him to death, or scream him into submission.

Wincing, the would-be robber reached back, caught her shoulder, and flipped her over his head. The next thing Sam knew, Ariel's behind was atop his face, her thighs pressed to his ears. Her dress had fluttered open and there was nothing more than a thin layer of silk keeping his nose from glory.

Damn it, why did things like this happen to him at all the wrong times?

Look for more Lori Foster in her holiday collection *Yule Be Mine*, on sale now!

With the sluggish winter sun hanging low in the gray sky, Detective Parker Ross dragged himself out of his salt-and-slush-covered car. Howling wind shoved against him, jerking the car door from his hand to slam it shut. His dress shoes slipped on the icy blacktop and he almost lost his footing. The frozen parking lot echoed his muttered curse.

Cautiously, he started forward, taking in the depressing sight of his apartment building. The landlord's attempts at decorating had left bedraggled strands of colored lights haphazardly tossed over the barren, neglected bushes that served as landscaping. Some of the bulbs had blown, while others blinked in a drunken hiccup.

On the ground near the walkway, a dented

plastic snowman lay on its side, half-covered in brownish slush, cigarette butts, and scraps of garbage.

Damn, but he'd be glad when the holidays passed and life returned to normal.

Slinging his soiled suit coat over his shoulder, his head down in exhaustion, Parker trudged along the treacherous, icy walkway. He didn't have an overcoat with him because the last perp he'd tangled with had destroyed it. Weariness and disgust kept him from noting the frozen snowflakes that gathered on the back of his neck; after such a bitch of a day, even the frigid December weather couldn't revive him.

A hot shower, some nuked food, and sleep— that's all he needed, in that exact order. Once he hit the sheets, he intended to stay there for a good ten hours. He had the next week off, and he didn't want to do anything more involved than camping on his couch and watching football.

God knew he deserved a rest. The past month of holiday-evoked lunacy and criminal desperation had left him little time for relaxation.

Parker saw Christmas as lavish, loud, and downright depressing. With his planned time off, he intended to hide out and avoid the nonsense.

Now, if he could just slip into his apartment without Lily Donaldson catching him . . .

Thinking of Lily sent a flood of warmth through his system, rejuvenating him in a way the frozen weather couldn't. He was old enough to know better, but no matter how he tried, Lily tempted him. She also infuriated him.

She aroused his curiosity, and his tenderness.

She made him think, and she made him hot.

She had trouble written all over her. *He* wanted to be all over her.

In the ten months he'd known her, Lily had influenced his life far too often. Smart, kind, gentle. She had carried food to Mrs. Harbinger when the old lady fell ill. She argued sound politics with fanatical Mr. Pitnosky. Both intelligent and astute, Lily smiled at everyone, never gossiped, and had a generous heart.

She *loved* Christmas, which rubbed him raw.

And she had a terrible case of hero worship. That was the hardest thing to deal with. Parker knew he didn't possess a single ounce of heroism. If he did, then resisting her wouldn't be so damn difficult.

In a hundred different ways, Lily made it clear she wanted to be more than friends. But her age made him wary, her enthusiasm scared him to death, and her love of a holiday he scorned showed they had little in common.

On top of all that, he had serious doubts about her occupation.

Yep, a conundrum for sure. Parker hated to think about it, yet he thought about it far too often. Not once had he ever noticed any work routine for Lily. Sure, she left her apartment, but not dressed for anything other than a real good time. Always made up. Always decked out, dressed for seduction.

Sometimes she left early, sometimes late.

Sometimes she stayed gone for days, and some days she never left the apartment at all. But that didn't stop a steady stream of admirers from calling on her. The only reason Parker could tolerate that situation was because the guys seldom lasted more than a few hours, never more than a day.

Whatever Lily did to support herself, she sure as hell didn't punch a time clock.

He'd tried asking her about her job a couple of times, but she always turned evasive and changed the subject, leaving Parker with few conclusions to draw.

He was a selfish bastard who refused to share, so even if the other roadblocks didn't exist, no way could he let their friendship grow into intimacy.

That didn't mean he could keep his mind off her. Throughout the awful day—hell, the awful *month*—thoughts of Lily made the hours more bearable. He imagined her sweet smile, the special one she saved for him. He imagined that deep admiration in her eyes whenever she looked at him.

He imagined her lush bod, minus the sexy clothes she wore.

Seeing her now would shove him right over the edge. Avoiding her was the smart thing to do.

He planned to duck inside as fast as his drained body would allow. If she knocked, and he knew she would, he'd pretend he wasn't home.

After rubbing his bloodshot eyes, he opened the entrance door to the apartment building and stepped inside. Whistling wind followed in his wake—and still he heard her husky voice, raised in ire.

Shit. With no way to reach his front door, Parker paused by the mailboxes and listened. Lily's usually sweet voice held a sharp edge of annoyance. She probably had another smitten swain who didn't want to take no for an answer.

Peering out the glass entrance doors, Parker considered a strategic retreat. Maybe he could drop by a bar and get a beer. Or visit his mother—*no, scratch that.* His mom would start trying to rope him in for a big family get-together, caroling, or God-knew-what-other holiday function.

Maybe he could . . .

Lily's voice grew more insistent, and Parker's protective instincts kicked in. Damn it, even if it fed her goofy misconceptions about him being heroic, he couldn't let some bozo hassle her. Giving up on the idea of escape, Parker trod the steps to the second floor. Halfway up he saw her, and he forgot to breathe.

A soft white sweater hugged her breasts. Dangling, beaded earrings in a snowflake design brushed her shoulders. Soft jeans accentuated a deliciously rounded ass.

Previously spent body parts perked up in attention. Nothing new there. No matter what Parker's brain tried to insist, his dick refused to pay attention.

Lily's pale blond hair, pinned up but with long tendrils teasing her nape and cheeks, gave the illusion that a lover had just finished with her. Heavily lashed brown eyes defied any innocence.

And her bare feet somehow made her look half-naked.

His heart picked up speed, sending needed blood flow into his lethargic muscles. Predictably enough, he went from exhausted to horny in a nanosecond.

Vibrating with annoyance, Lily stood just outside her apartment. A fresh, decorated wreath hung from her door, serving as a festive backdrop.

Lily loved the holiday. And he loathed it.

But for now, he couldn't let that matter. Lily had a problem. She had a dispute.

She had . . . *a guy on his knees?*

Parker blinked in surprise at that. Lily's confrontations always involved men. More specifically, they involved Lily rejecting men. But a begging guy?

That was a first.

Glued to his spot on the stairs, Parker stared, and listened.

"It was *not* a date, Clive. Not ever. No way. I made that clear."

"But we had lunch," Clive insisted, reaching out to grasp her knee. "Just the two of us."

While stepping back, out of reach, Lily exclaimed, "I picked up the bill!"

Clive crawled after her. "But I would have."

She slapped his hands away. "I didn't let you—*because it was not a date.*"

"Lily," he moaned. "I thought we had something special."

"Tuna fish on rye is not special, Clive. Now *get up.*"

At her surly reply, Parker bit back a smile. Lily excelled in brokenhearted boyfriends, and this guy looked very brokenhearted. Poor schmuck.

As Clive obediently climbed to his feet, Parker looked at Lily—and met her gaze. The surprise in her brown eyes softened to pleasure; she gave him a silly, relieved smile—expecting him to heroically save the day.

And Parker supposed he would.

He'd taken one step toward her when good old Clive threw his arms around her. "I love you!"

"Oh, *puh-lease.*" Lily shoved against him, but Clive wouldn't let go.

"I do," he insisted. "Let me show you how much."

Glancing toward Parker, Lily said, "Don't be stupid, Clive. I know why you're here."

Parker knew why, too. Lily was sexy and sweet, and Clive wanted in her pants.

"You're after my money," Lily stated, causing Parker to do a double take.

"Lily, no!" Clive cried.

"You're broke, Clive. I know all about your business going under, the losses you've sustained."

"Temporary setbacks, I swear."

"Right. Temporary, because you figured I could shore you back up." She leaned away from Clive's hold.

"*Noooo.*" Clive tugged her close again.

Straightening her arms to hold Clive off, Lily looked at Parker. "Well, don't just stand there."

Smirking, Parker took the remaining steps to

the landing and caught Clive by the back of his coat. Because he was tired and annoyed—and damn it, he didn't like seeing other men slobbering on Lily—Parker rattled him.

"The lady said to leave." For good measure, he shook Clive again before setting him several feet away from Lily. "Now beat it."

Flustered, Clive straightened his coat with righteous anger. "Who the hell are you?"

"Just a neighbor."

"Then this doesn't concern you."

Given his height of six feet four, Parker had the advantage of looking down on most people, especially shorter people like Clive. "I'm a cop. I've had a shitty day." He leaned toward Clive, forcing him to back up. "I've dealt with a three-car pileup. Got knocked into a damn curb full of blackened slush by a mob of *happy* shoppers. Got jumped by a crazy woman stealing a bike for her kid. Had to break up a riot during a TV sale. *And* wrestled with a goon robbing Santa of donations for the homeless. I am *not* in the mood to tell you twice."

Clive gulped. "I just need to explain to her . . ."

"She's not interested in your explanations."

Lily moved to stand beside Parker. "No, I'm not." She curled her arms around one of his for no reason that Parker could find. She did that a lot. If she spoke to him, she touched him—almost as if she couldn't help herself.

And it drove him nuts.

"All right." Dejected, Clive fashioned a puppy-dog face. "But you're making a mistake, Lily. I do love you. With all my heart." He turned and slunk down the stairs like a man on the way to the gallows.

When the door closed behind Clive, Parker mustered up his good sense and peeled Lily's hands off his arm. "Good night, Lily." He headed for his door.

"Good night?" She hustled after him. "But . . . what do you mean, 'good night'?"

"I'm beat. It's been a hell of a day." Parker refused to look at her. Just being near her made him twitchy in the pants. If he looked at her, he'd be a goner.

"Sounds like." She scuttled in front of him, blocking his way. "I never realized that detectives got into so many physical confrontations."

That damned admiring tone weakened his resolve. "It's the holidays." He couldn't help but look at her, and once he did, he couldn't look away. "It brings out the worst in everyone."

Gently, Lily said, "That's not true."

His day had been just bad enough to shatter his resolve. He wanted to vent. To Lily. Somehow, he knew she'd understand.

To disguise his level of emotion, Parker snorted. "The wreck I mentioned? It sent two innocent people to the hospital."

Concern clouded her beautiful eyes. "I'm so sorry to hear that."

"I got called in because the arresting officer found psilocybin mushrooms in the car of the idiot who caused the wreck. Enough to know he's a dealer."

"Hallucinogenic drugs," Lily breathed, surprising Parker. "How terrible. Will the victims be all right?"

Parker eyed her. What the hell did Lily know about mushrooms? "I don't know," he grouched. "Last I heard, the woman was in surgery." She had two kids who'd be counting on her to be there Christmas morning. Parker hoped like hell she made it.

"The dealer?"

"Escaped without a scratch."

"But you'll see to him, I'm sure."

Parker ground his teeth together, pissed off all over again. Lily sounded so confident in his ability. "I'd already arrested him once on a charge of manufacturing methamphetamine, but he failed to appear in court. At least this should cinch a conviction."

Lily inched closer, her expression sympathetic, her mood nurturing. "Your job isn't often an easy one, is it?"

Damn, she looked sweet and soft, and far too appealing. Parker cleared his throat. "Look, Lily, I'm beat. I don't want to talk about work." He didn't want to tempt himself with her. "I need to get some shut-eye."

Her hand settled over his, her fingers warm and gentle. "At least let me explain about Clive."

Cocking a brow, Parker said, "It was pretty self-explanatory."

Leaning on the wall beside his door, her gaze somber, she studied him. "I had no idea Clive harbored an infatuation. He said he wanted to talk about business, my schedule was clear..." She shut down on that real fast. "It was not an intimate lunch."

The nature of their business made Parker's stomach roil. "So you said."

"I guess you got an earful, huh?" She didn't sound all that embarrassed. "He lied to me, Parker, saying he wanted to help with a project of mine, telling me he wanted to be friends. Can you believe his nerve?"

"The world is full of creeps, Lily." What project? No, he didn't care. "Good night."

Lily's voice dropped. "It's barely six o'clock."

Sticking his key in the lock, Parker tried to ignore her nearness. An impossible task. "I've been up for over twenty-four hours. I can't see straight anymore. Fast as I can get a shower and find some food, I'll be turning in." His door opened. He stepped inside...

Lily followed. "Poor baby." She touched him again, this time on his right biceps.

Even through his shirt, Parker felt the tingling jolt that shot through his system and fired up his gonads. She might as well have grabbed his crotch for the way it affected him.

Unaware of his rioting libido, Lily said, "I feel terrible that you got pulled into the middle of my mess after all you've been through today."

Before he could censor himself, Parker said, "It's getting to be a habit."

Lily tilted her head and smiled. "I can think of worse habits than drawing your attention."

Please don't go there. "Sorry." Parker ran a hand over the knotted muscles in his neck. "I didn't mean that the way it sounded."

"I understand. I . . . I do seem to have a bad track record with guys."

"Lily . . ."

"I don't blame myself, though." Rather than explain, she brightened her smile and changed the subject. "Now that Clive's gone, why don't you let me thank you with dinner?"

Parker took a step back, then stopped to curse himself. Damn it, since when did women have him retreating like a green kid in middle school?

Since Lily had moved in—smelling, looking, probably tasting like sex.